Jesús Salvador Treviño

Arte Público Press
Houston, Texas

Return to Arroyo Grande is funded in part by grants from the city of Houston through the Houston Arts Alliance and the National Endowment for the Arts. We are grateful for their support.

Recovering the past, creating the future

Arte Público Press
University of Houston
4902 Gulf Fwy, Bldg 19, Rm 100
Houston, Texas 77204-2004

Cover art by Wayne Healy, "Métete o te meto"
Cover design by Mora Des!gn

Treviño, Jesús Salvador.
[Short stories. Selections]
Return to Arroyo Grande / by Jesús Salvador Treviño.
p. cm.
Includes bibliographical references and index.
ISBN 978-1-55885-819-0 (alk. paper)
I. Title.
PS3570.R445A6 2015
813'.54—dc23

2015034243
CIP

♾ The paper used in this publication meets the requirements of the American National Standard for Information Sciences—Permanence of Paper for Printed Library Materials, ANSI Z39.48-1984.

15 16 17 18 19 20 8 7 6 5 4 3 2 1

Table of Contents

"Any resemblance of persons depicted in these fictional stories to real people, alive or not, of course, is purely coincidental."

To the literary pioneers who showed us the way
and continue to lead. And you know who you are.

WHERE LOST OBJECTS RESIDE

News of Old Man Baldemar's death swept through Arroyo Grande faster than the eighty-mile winds that had propitiously swept through the West Texas town four years earlier, bringing an end to a drought and resurrecting its citizens from a rare insomnia that had hijacked the town's sleeping habits for months.

While everyone seemed to agree the grumpy septuagenarian's mortal soul no longer remained on God's earth, the exact cause of his demise seemed to be less a matter of public record and more of a contagious rumor.

Max Martínez told Rosalinda Rodríguez, who had brought in her computer to the WE FIX ANYTHING shop for repairs, the old coot had died of a sudden onset of pneumonia. Baldemar's perennial coughing and wheezing was legendary. Across town, Don Carlos Vásquez told the construction crew foreman working at the new downtown convention center that the old geezer was hit by a car when he was crossing Main Street. The Maldonado Brothers posted a large notice outside their garage announcing that Baldemar's death was due to "a prolonged bout with the big C." Rolando Hinojosa, who just had completed yet another book in his Klail City Death trip series, announced to all present at the weekly meeting of the Querétaro Literary Society that the perverse recluse had been accidentally electrocuted while trying to rewire his decrepit wood frame house.

At the early Sunday Mass at St. Anthony's, Father Ronquillo intoned with great sadness and the absolute certainty characteristic of clergy that "our dearly beloved neighbor, Eufemio Constantino Baldemar, has passed into the Creator's hands due to cardiac arrest." And Terri Wilja, the clerk at the Arroyo Grande post office, told patrons the foul-mouthed curmudgeon had died from a stroke after a particularly violent outburst of cursing.

And me?

I got the news from Terri Butler as I returned to Arroyo Grande after seeing Choo Choo off at the El Paso airport for his connecting flight to Phoenix and then on to Los Angeles—Choo Choo was off to college at USC! I was *rete triste* not just because Choo Choo was gone, but because I was the only Slugger still left in limbo. Everyone else from our childhood baseball team had been accepted to college or had secured a well-paying job away from Arroyo Grande. They all had a future.

As for me, I had received rejection notices from five of the schools to which I had applied (Yale, Carnegie Mellon, CalArts, Pratt Institute and the Rhode Island School of Design). The only one I hadn't heard from was the Parson School of Design in New York, which had always seemed like a longshot. As soon as I got *that* rejection, then I'd really have to face the ugly truth: at eighteen, Yoli Mendoza was a total loser destined to spend the rest of her life bagging groceries at the Arroyo Grande Supermart.

At first, Terri Butler's words didn't register when she stuck her head out the door of the Mesquite Book Store and yelled out to me, "Yoli! Yoli! Have you heard the news? Old Man Baldemar died this morning!"

"What?" I asked, still too caught up in my personal angst for the news to sink in.

"Old Man Baldemar!" Terri insisted, depositing her cat, Juniper, onto its favorite sunning spot on the amply lit, tile-decorated window ledge of the bookstore. "He up and died this morning. Don't you buy groceries for him each week?"

"*¡Híjole!*" I exclaimed as the information suddenly penetrated my dense noggin. Not only was my weekly job of buying Old Man Baldemar's groceries suddenly at an abrupt end, but more importantly, I wondered about El Gordo and El Flaco, the old reprobate's parakeets. The poor babies, what would become of them?

"Oh, thanks Terri," I said. "I gotta check on El Gordo y El Flaco!"

I raced from the downtown plaza and onto Calle Cuatro, where Old Man Baldemar lived. My gosh, I hoped the parakeets were all right!

El Gordo and El Flaco were the Spanish names given to the old comedy team of Laurel and Hardy. Old Man Baldemar, with his wacky humor, had christened his two pet parakeets by the same names. Because of his rheumatoid arthritis, he could no longer do his own shopping, and so he paid me handsomely to buy feed for his birds and groceries for him from the lengthy list he compiled for me every Friday morning. Since I worked five hours every day as a bagger at the Arroyo Grande Supermart, buying his groceries was easy. I did it during my lunch break and delivered them to him after work.

I gotta admit it had taken a little courage for me to agree to work for Old Man Baldemar when he first approached me. He had a reputation for being a mean, foul-mouthed recluse. I remember once, when a bunch of us Arroyo Grande Sluggers had crossed through his back yard as a shortcut to baseball practice, he had come out and thrown rocks at us! He cursed us and told us to stay the hell away from his house. Nonetheless, I had agreed to take the job. And it had worked out well for me.

But now Old Man Baldemar was dead! What would become of his two birds? And what about my job? I had counted on the job to help get me through the summer cutbacks in hours at the Supermart. What would I do when I got the Parsons rejection? That would confirm the truth I didn't want to face—I was not destined for a career as an artist. Geez, my future was up in the air more than ever!

* * *

A few minutes later, I arrived at the creaky porch of Old Man Baldemar's tiny, wood-frame house. Everything seemed to be in order—the same flaking paint, sagging porch studs and that stinky couch with the springs showing through the cushion seats. It was quite a sight, but I had become used to it as the depository for the notes he always left me.

Baldemar would write out the list of groceries he needed and leave them in an envelope on the weathered couch, and I'd pick it up on my way to school. He always had an envelope waiting for me with my weekly pay in it. Always in his carefully written hand: *For Yolanda Mendoza. Open at once!* I always thought that was a little melodramatic—Open at once? Really!

Out of habit, I knocked on the front door. Then I realized if he was dead, they must have already taken him away and he wasn't going answer the door. I looked around and saw that *somebody* had been there. There were remnants of police tape on the porch, and a lot of muddy shoe prints and several empty Styrofoam coffee cups. It was then that I noticed a hastily written note on the door reading, "To whom it may concern: Mr. Baldemar passed away this morning. An investigation into the details of his death is pending."

I thought that maybe I should leave. Surely whoever was investigating his death would have seen the birds in the kitchen and would have made some kind of arrangements. I was convinced that the Arroyo Grande police would have taken them over to the SPCA. But what if they hadn't? What if the birds were still in the kitchen where Old Man Baldemar kept them, and what if they had no water or food?

I was such a coward. I knew in my heart of hearts I should just go into the house and check on the birds. But instead I sat on the steps of the front porch for a good five minutes, trying to build up my courage.

I heard the phone inside the house ringing.

Who could it be? Did the old reprobate have friends who might call him? Probably a bill collector or one of those phone solicitors. I started to leave but a wave of guilt swept over me. Shouldn't I, at least, answer the phone? What if it was a family member that didn't know what had happened to him. Didn't he or she deserve to know what had transpired? Yes, maybe I should go in and answer the phone. Wasn't that the Christian thing to do? And then, as if on cue, I heard El Flaco and El Gordo chirping up a storm inside the house. They must have heard me on the porch or heard the phone ringing. Yes, they were definitely in the house. Well, that did it! I wasn't going to jeopardize the lives of his birds. I made my way back to the front door and tried the handle. To my surprise, the door squeaked open.

I entered the living room. Old Man Baldemar had never let me—nor anyone else for that matter—set foot inside the house. He was always pretty clear about that. "Just leave the groceries and the bird food on the porch. You'll find an envelope there with your pay." Yeah, it was a little mysterious, but that worked fine with me. So it was a little scary stepping into this ancient, musty house for the first time. Judging from the aged adobe walls, the house might well have been there when Arroyo Grande itself was founded more than four hundred years ago. I mean, that certainly could be—the walls were made of white-washed thick adobe.

I entered the living room and quickly realized what I was hearing was not just one phone, but several—two, three, perhaps a dozen! Now that was really odd! I followed the sound into an adjacent hallway. The hallway was a real surprise, because from the outside the house looked like it might contain all of three or four rooms—a really tiny little barrio house. But once inside, the house seemed enormous.

I followed the long hallway—geez it was twenty feet long! All the time trying to figure in my mind how such a lengthy corridor could fit inside the house that looked so tiny from the outside? I passed a closed door on my right, and then a closed door on my left and then I found a door from which the ringing phone seemed to be emanating. I placed my hand on the doorknob and felt a weird kind of thrill. My gosh, it sounded like all the phones in the world were inside. I opened the door and walked in. I just stopped—stood there with my eyes wide open and goose bumps inching along my spine.

Oh, my Gaaahd!

The room looked like something out of a high tech nerve center. There were dozens and dozens of thin metallic shelves, one right above the other, each separated by no more than four or five inches. Shelf upon shelf upon shelf, all the way to the ceiling. And arranged neatly on each shelf were dozens and dozens, heck there were hundreds of cell phones, all of them blaring away! I walked to the nearest desk and picked up one of the cell phones. I saw that it had a label attached with a small piece of twine. On the label it said, "Hank Thompson, Toledo, Ohio, Sept 21, 2001."

What I did came natural. I answered it.

"Hello?" I said into the phone.

The ringing stopped. There was silence at the other end. I put the phone down and it began to ring again. I saw that each phone on the shelf had a tag on it, each with a name, a city and state and a date. And not all of the cities where in the United States. Many of the cell phone listed cities in other countries.

"Joel Juárez, June 24, 1999, Valladolid, Spain."

"Kenton Youngstrom, Olso, Norway, October 17, 1996."

"Kirk Whistler, January 17, 2007, Manchester, England."

"Ng'ethe Maina, May 22, 2004, Nairobi, Kenya."

The list went on and on. I took a step back and took a deep breath. What did all of this mean?

I got spooked, so I decided to leave the room. I walked out and closed the door behind me and just stood there a moment. To my surprise, the ringing stopped!

I opened the door and looked inside. The cell phones were still there, but the ringing had stopped. Wow, it was really spooky.

I turned and looked across the hall at the first door I had passed. I couldn't resist it. I opened the door and if my surprise at the first room had blown me away, this one really knocked me inside out. It was an enormous room, with comfortable stuffed chairs, wood paneled shelves and elegant wooden bureaus and ancient roll-top desks, at least a half dozen of them! I pulled out a drawer of one and there, neatly arranged, were rows upon rows of gold wedding bands. Yes, and each wedding ring had a tag attached with a name, a city of origin and a date. I could see that some of these rings were really old. Some were dated in the 1700s and 1800s!

"Kay Brown, February 2, 1881, Salt Lake City, Utah."

"Enrique La Salle, August 6, 1898, Vienna, Austria."

"Isadora Melencamp, December 26, 1932, Augusta, Georgia."

That's when I lost it. I plopped down on the floor—there were absolutely no chairs in the room—and wrapped my arms around my legs and just rocked back and forth. Speechless. I had to think this out.

Was I going crazy? Was I having some kind of psychotic episode? A delusion? Was this a waking dream? It certainly *felt* like a dream. But when I pinched myself, it really hurt! This was no dream. I was really seeing things that should not be, or that at least were mighty, mighty weird. Well, then, I thought, if it is a dream, then go with it. What else could be in the other rooms of this crazy, wacky house?

I walked down the hallway. The third door contained a room full of sunglasses—all kinds and varieties, all colors and hues, all sizes and styles. And, yep! Each one had a tiny tag attached with a name, a city and a date.

The next door opened into a room that looked like a kitchen. Inside, adorned with lovely yellow flower wallpaper and trim blue curtains, were trays and trays of plastic ware lids. Square lids and round lids, and octagonal lids, blue, red, orange and clear plastic, all stacked one on another so that the entire room was overflowing with different sized plastic ware. And on each plastic lid was a person's name, the name of a city and a date.

I closed the door behind me and saw the second hallway. At the end of the first hallway, I entered a right corridor which I thought led to a back door. But instead it was a second hallway, and this one was at least thirty feet long! And, yes, each side of the hallway was lined with closed doors on both sides.

I walked down the hallway and at the end of the corridor made a turn, and the two hallways split off, each in a different direction! And at the end of each of these hallways, yes, my gosh, there appeared to be others! A fourth and a fifth and sixth hallway.

How could all of them, all of them, fit into this tiny house? It was physically impossible! And yet my very eyes told me it was true! And in each hallway, there were doors upon doors leading to countless rooms. None of this was possible if the laws of physics, geometry and logic that I had learned at Jefferson High School made any sense at all.

For the next hour I wandered from room to room. The hallways were endless. I'd open a door and inside I'd see a basement workroom, filled with screw drivers—all sorts and all sizes. Another door revealed a sitting room, filled with elegant bureaus and desks, and in each drawer, rows and rows of eyeglasses. A roomful of watches, all sizes, models and colors—some going back two or three hundred years! A room full of socks, but not pairs of socks, just single socks and of different colors, different sizes, different styles—men's socks, women's socks, children's socks. In another room, I found countless credit cards—from hundreds of credit companies, department stores and banks. In another room, car keys; in another room, wallets; in another room, hand guns; in another room, kitchen utensils. On and on.

I found only one room with the door locked. An engraved sign on the door read INCINERATOR.

Most surprising, there was one door with a hand-scrawled note—I could tell it was Old Man Baldemar's hand-writing. The note said, "Left over items from the Sinkhole. To be retained for future use." I opened the door and inside was a roomful of odd objects: a claw hammer, a three-peso Cuban note, a New York auto license. Then I remembered where I had seen these items before. These were some of the items that had been pulled up from the sinkhole in Mrs. Romero's front yard a few years ago. The same sinkhole where I had gotten my tube of Xenosium, which I had kept so secret all of these years. That hit close to home. I closed the door and ran back to the living room where I had entered. And then I suddenly remembered what had brought me in here in the first place—El Gordo and El Flaco!

I rushed into the adjacent kitchen to find the two parakeets in the cage that Old Man Baldemar had pulled from Mrs. Romero's sinkhole. They were chirping away, as if nothing had happened, as if my whole world hadn't just been turned upside down by what I'd seen. I quickly fed the birds—yes, they were hungry!—and then went back into the living and sat down. I finally put my thoughts together and tried to make sense of what I had seen in each room.

I consider myself a pragmatist and heck, maybe even an empiricist. Okay, I can be a little romantic and I do believe in true love and things like that. But when it comes to life situations, I go with what my senses tell me—sight, sound, touch, hearing, smelling. But my logic told me certain things could not be. I realized I needed to confirm what my senses appeared to be telling me.

I walked outside and paced off the length of the front of the house, putting one foot directly in front of the other. Each foot was slightly shorter than twelve inches, but I figured it still would be a good estimate. Porch included, the front of the house was about twenty-five paces or twenty-five feet across. Next, I paced off the side of the house. From the outside of the house there appeared to be only two rooms visible, two windows, located behind the main living room area behind the front door. The side of the house appeared to be about forty feet in length on each side. I went back to the front of the house and drew a diagram of a rectangle on a piece of paper—twenty-five feet on one side and forty feet on the other.

Then, diagram in hand, I walked back into the house. I paced my way down the first hallway and into the next, and then continued walking into a third hallway. After I had walked a distance of about 100 feet, it was clear to me that the inside of the house had nothing to do with the exterior. I sat down again and thought about that for a while.

My conclusion was obvious. Either I was completely deranged, with my senses confirming for me things that were completely impossible, or I had walked into the greatest mystery of my life and possibly the entire world.

As near as I could figure, Old Man Baldemar's house appeared to be filled with items that had been lost—at some point in time, in some city, in some country, by some person—objects that ran the gamut from eyeglasses to wedding rings, to wallets, to tools, to clothing, to the dozens and dozens of objects that people inevitably misplace, desert, dismiss, abandon or otherwise automatically lose in the course of the daily hustle and bustle of life. And somehow they had all ended up here in this house in Arroyo Grande that on the outside appeared to be a typical barrio residence but that, in fact, was limitless in size inside!

And Old Man Baldemar was responsible for all of this in some way! Yes! Suddenly I got it. *That's* why he had been so antisocial all of these years. That's why he yelled at all us kids to keep away. He was keeping the biggest secret in Arroyo Grande to himself.

But now he was gone. Dead. And what would become of the house? And of all of those objects?

That's when I noticed an old cardboard shoe box next to the birdcage. Inside was an envelope nestled in among a pile of tags like the ones I had seen on the objects in the various rooms. Except there were no objects in the box, just a pile of tags. I picked up the envelope and immediately recognized the writing on it. It was the same type of envelope the old coot used to pay my weekly salary. But now the words carried a meaning they had never had for me before: *For Yolanda Mendoza. Open Immediately!* And, of course, I did!

* * *

"Max, what does it mean?"

The next morning I sat with Max Martínez on the porch of Old Man Baldemar's house. After reading the contents of the letter addressed to me, I decided I needed a legal advice. Max Martínez, who ran the WE FIX ANYTHING repair shop, wasn't exactly an attorney, but he was the best-read man in Arroyo Grande. And the truth was that I trusted his legal advice much more so than any of the professional "esquires" whose offices lined Main Street in Arroyo Grande. After first making him swear to secrecy, I told him what I had found at Baldemar's place. He agreed to review the letter for me but insisted on seeing the peculiar rooms of the house for himself.

I took him into the house and showed him several of the hallways and rooms. His eyes just kept getting bigger and bigger each time we opened a door and looked inside. Finally, he stopped. "I need some fresh air," he said, walked outside and collapsed on the musty couch with the sagging seats.

"We'll get to the letter in a minute," he said. "Right now, I got to figure out what it is I just saw."

He turned to look at the front of the house and then stepped down from the porch and started walking around the house, carefully counting off his paces as he walked.

"Max, I've already done that," I said, showing him my diagram.

He looked at it carefully. "And you also paced out . . . " he began.

"Inside, there's at least six corridors we walked through just now, for a total of at least two hundred feet. *De veras*, it just defies the laws of physics!"

"Sure does," he said, sitting back onto the couch. "Hmm."

Then he read the letter Old Man Baldemar had left for me. He read it over and over several times. Finally, he made a bubble with his mouth, blew out the air and spoke.

"Well, it's a contract."

"Max, I know that!" I said, exasperated. "*That's* why I bought it to you!"

"Hmm," he said, examining the one-page contract even more closely. "Yeah," he reiterated, "it sure looks like a contract to me. Concise and to the point." He read from the paper:

> *I, Yolanda Mendoza, residing at ____________________), in the community of Arroyo Grande, Texas, United States of America, do agree that upon the demise of Eufemio Constantino Baldemar (hereafter known as the Caretaker), to assume the responsibilities, tasks and duties associated with the position of Caretaker of the residence at 713 Fourth Street, Arroyo Grande, Texas (hereafter known as the Residence) for the standard compensation associated with the profession and to do all in my power to oversee, catalog, archive, administer and protect and return, when appropriate, all the valuable artifacts, objects and miscellanea therein contained. Notwithstanding the peculiarity of the office, I do state that I am of sound mind and body, fully empowered to execute this agreement, understand the long range, cumulative, life-altering and irrevocable implications of my decision. Further, I attest that for good and valuable consideration not herein described but acknowledged by both*

parties, I agree to assume the obligations herein referenced, to be fully executed in a conscientious manner, in good faith, and to the best of my human ability in perpetuity, for all eternity or should I leave the job, on my demise.

*Signed*_________________________*Dated*____________.

Countersigned: Caretaker, Euphemio Constantino Baldemar.

"Humph," Max muttered to himself. "Pretty good legal writing! And he did sign it."

"Max," I implored, "What does it mean to me? What should I do? '*For standard compensation associated with the profession* . . . .' What compensation? And what about '*long range, cumulative, life-altering and irrevocable implications of my decision*'? That sounds downright scary! What does he mean, '*return?*' To whom and how?"

"Hmmm. Trying to make sense of this. Yoli, did you ever speak with Old Man Baldemar about any kind of compensation other than what he paid you to pick up the groceries?"

"Absolutely not."

"'*For good and valuable consideration*,'" Max read out loud, "'*not herein described but acknowledged by both parties* . . . ' And you never made any other kind of deal with him, didn't necessarily agree to anything, but maybe something that was implied . . . anything?"

Okay, that stopped me for a moment. Suddenly I remembered the very strange conversation I'd had with Old Man Baldemar a few weeks earlier.

"Well, there was a kind of a weird conversation we had not long ago," I confessed, reluctant to divulge much more.

"Well?" Max pressured, "Tell me about it."

"Oh, I'm sure it was nothing."

"Yoli, if you want me to help, you got to tell me everything."

"Okay, okay! A few weeks ago, I had delivered the groceries as usual, left them on the porch on this stinky couch. I was about to leave, when Old Man Baldemar came out. He's usually pretty tight-lipped, so I was surprised to see him wanting to talk. He asked me about the other kids and what was going to happen now that we were all graduated. He knew most of us since we were seven or eight years old. So I told him about where everyone was going, now that we were all graduated, and how I was still waiting to hear from Parsons School of Design.

"I noticed he had a brochure in his hand and asked him about it. Turned out it was a travel brochure for a trip to Machu Picchu. 'Ever since I pulled this out of Mrs. Romero's sinkhole,' he told me, 'I've had a dream of leaving Arroyo Grande and visiting Machu Picchu, and, for that matter, all of Latin America. Seeing the world while I still can.'

"'Why don't you?' I asked, suddenly regretting the words that came out of my mouth. I knew he sustained himself on his meager pension and from the way he lived, I thought there was not a lot of money left over. Besides, there was his health.

"'It's not the money,' he said, reading my mind. 'Believe it or not, I've salted some dough away. But I got responsibilities here that would make any trip like that impossible, and of course my arthritis. You're lucky, you're young, you can still travel and do what you want.'

"'Not likely,' I said, suddenly sad. He had hit on my deepest insecurity, what was I going to do if I were rejected by Parsons? 'If I don't get accepted by Parsons, it'll be the end of my so-called art career. When five schools turn you down, that's life's way of saying, you're not much of an artist. I'll be stuck here in Arroyo Grande bagging groceries at the Supermart.'

"'Nothing else going for you, eh?' he asked.

"'Not a thing,' I told him bitterly.

"'I had heard that you and that young man Choo Choo Torres were going to be wed?'

"'Broke it off,' I told him.

"I didn't want to get into *that* whole saga. How we had broken off the engagement when Choo Cho said he had to pursue a career in filmmaking at all costs. And me, I couldn't just let him put me aside. So I had said, yes, let's call off the wedding. I have a career in art waiting for me! Except, of course, I didn't.

"*¡Híjole!* I didn't know how much pent up anger I had inside until that moment with Old Man Baldemar. I suddenly opened up to the old man. 'The highlight of her life was high school, after that she settled into an uninspired life of boredom in Arroyo Grande going from useless job to useless job until she got old and died.'

"'You want to do something special with your life,' he asked.

"'Doesn't everyone?' I replied.

"'What if you had a chance to do something unique, a job that would benefit all of humankind? But a job for which you might not get any recognition? Would you take such a job?'

"'Sounds like being a nun? Sure, anything but spending my life as a bagger at the Supermart!' I told him.

"That's when I couldn't take it anymore. I quickly said goodbye to Old Man Baldemar and ran off. That's it. That was our conversation."

"Hmmm," said Max. "Well, that may have something to do with this line here about *'for good and valuable consideration acknowledged by both parties.'*"

"I don't follow."

"It seems to me that Old Man Baldemar is offering you something very inspiring, something that would truly make your life important."

"This caretaker job? I don't even understand it."

"Yeah, that's the part that has me stumped."

"Hello, that's the part that I came for you to clarify! I mean, I haven't made any deal or anything. And so far there's absolutely no indication of what I am being compensated for if I do agree to take on this stupid job of being a caretaker for other people's carelessness."

"Wait a minute! This is deep," he said, scratching at his goatee. "This is about you assuming the guilt of the world, or at least the carelessness of others, and making amends."

"Huh?" I said.

"Look at it this way. Throughout the world, millions of people are inattentive each day. They forget their watches, their sunglasses, their cell phones, their wedding rings. Whatever. They lose them. In a universe that abhors a vacuum, a universe of cosmic balance, all of these items need to be accounted for. And that would be your job. Keeping order in the universe. Keeping the cosmic balance, life in harmony with itself!"

"And that's what you think this job is about . . . caretaker of the world's junk?"

"There's more," Max said, "the contract also says '*return*.'"

"Yeah?"

"That shoe box you mentioned. Let me see it."

I brought the box over. He looked in and started pulling out tags, examining each carefully. "Humm," he said, "and there were no objects in the box?"

"Nothing but the tags."

"But where did the objects to which these tags were once attached go?"

What was Max getting at? I wondered.

"Ah hah!" Max said, as if he had just been hit on the head with an apple and discovered the laws of physics. "*That's* what this is about. '*Return*' means you liberate these objects, you return them to their rightful owners."

"I don't get it," I told Max. And I meant it.

"Yoli, without this house, without this place, things stay lost. Old Man Baldemar is offering you a job. To see to it that all those things that people lose eventually get back to them. Obviously it doesn't always happen. I mean people lose things and sometimes they never turn up. But you also hear about that letter that was sent to someone in the 1940s and they finally find it now. Or that wedding ring that was lost until the plumbers opened up the clogged kitchen pipes and found it. That all must be the work of Old Man Baldemar."

"Oh is it, really?" I said, trying to keep the sarcasm out of my voice.

"I think that's the job he's offering you. To return objects to the rightful people to whom they belong—when and if it's the right time."

"Or to destroy them," I said, suddenly getting an insight.

"Huh?" Max said.

I told Max about the incinerator room, which he hadn't seen.

"That sounds about right," he agreed. "Not all things in life need to be remembered or returned to their owners. It's better some things are forgotten, you toss them into the incinerator. He's asking you to assume the responsibility of being the caretaker of these objects. Gosh, it's, it's, geez, Christ-like!"

"What?!!"

"It's an honor. You know, like Christ died for your sins and all of that. Well, here you are being asked to assume the load of people's carelessness and irresponsibility! And no one will ever know about it but you! I tell you this is really deep!"

"Max, what do I get in return? Why should I even give this offer a second thought?"

"I think he's offering you immortality, that's why."

"What?"

"The contract says 'for all eternity or, should I leave the job, on my demise.' As I read it, you'll never die as long as you are the caretaker."

Immortality? I savored the idea. Wow, living forever?

"Something to think about for sure. But here's this phone number at the bottom of the contract. Maybe you should call it and find out your options."

"Phone number?" I said, taking the contract from his hands. I looked down at the bottom of the page and, sure enough, in very small print a phone number was listed. Why hadn't I seen that before?

* * *

That night I couldn't sleep. I tossed and turned. My dreams were confusing and frightening. In one dream Old Man Baldemar yelled at me, "You must sign the contract!" and then Choo Choo came out of nowhere, camera in hand, saying "Yoli, are you seriously considering this? You must be nuts!" And then I yelled at Choo Choo, "You can talk, you got accepted at USC! What about me? You deserted me!" I finally woke up in the early morning and couldn't sleep anymore.

As I made my morning coffee, I realized that this whole episode with Baldemar's house had forced me to face the question that I had been avoiding as I planned for my future. Was I really cut out to be an artist? Did I have what it takes? Did I have any talent at all, or was I just kidding myself? The words of my father at the dinner table a few weeks ago still rang in my mind, "*M'ija*, forget your art ideas. You need to plan for something practical. Be a nurse, a computer programmer. *Algo práctico*."

I had dreamed of being an artist since I had pulled that all-too-curious sketch pad out of Mrs. Romero's sinkhole, and, of course, the tube of Xenosium. And all through high school I took every art course that was offered. I even volunteered to work on the mural that Carlos Callejo, a local El Paso artist, had painted in the old town square depicting Arroyo Grande's history. But the steady rejections from all those art schools had worn away my self-esteem and confidence.

I brewed a cup of coffee, trying not make a lot of noise. It was Saturday morning, the one morning my dad was able to sleep in. As I sipped my coffee, I finally came to a conclusion. No matter what, I was going to be an artist! No matter what!

Once the decision was made, the rest was easy. I knew then that I had to call the phone number on the letter Old Man Baldemar had left me. The phone rang only once and a voice came on. It was Old Man Baldemar's gruff voice on the phone, "You have reached the right number. If your answer is yes, please sign the document and leave it in the shoebox at the house. You'll get further instructions. If your answer is no, then return the contract to the house, put it on the kitchen table, lock the door and best of luck to you in your future plans."

Well, that certainly placed everything in perspective.

I returned to Old Man Baldemar's house, contract in hand, with a great sense of relief. I knew now what to do and went about it methodically, efficiently and thoroughly. First, I bundled up the cage with El Gordo and El Flaco and took it to my mother, who agreed to become the new parent of the two birds. Then I proceeded to clean out all the trash from Baldemar's kitchen—food, anything that could go bad. I threw it all in the trash cans for Arroyo Grande sanitation to haul away. I did a last inspection of the house before I headed out. I placed the contract on the kitchen table and then heard a voice behind me.

"Have you really made up your mind?"

I jumped at the voice and turned to see who was behind me. It seemed my heart stopped beating for an eternity. There, standing in front of me at the kitchen door was none other than Old Man Baldemar himself! Not dead at all, but very much alive!

"*¡Híjole!* You're not dead!"

"Do I look like I'm dead? What's all this about me being dead, anyway? Dead? Who told you that?"

"*Everyone* said you were dead. And there was the police tape and the sign."

"Well, this should teach you not to believe in what everyone says. As you can see, I'm standing right here in front of you and not dead at all."

He sat down in one of his dilapidated chairs, the kind with the metal legs and plastic seat covers. "Truth is," he chuckled, "I started the rumor myself—just wanted to go away for a little while."

I sat down at the table opposite him. I could feel my eyes starting to tear up. I blinked away the tears. I don't know where they came from.

"You started the rumor! Well, where have you been all of this time?"

"Well, if you must know, I went here." He handed me the faded brochure and travel guide to Machu Picchu he had shown me not so long ago.

"You went to Machu Picchu?"

"Short trip. It wasn't what I expected. The altitude really got to me. And you *not* taking the job I offered, well, I didn't expect that either. I thought you'd jump at the chance. I guess I read you wrong, eh?"

"Yes, you did. Really, Mr. Baldemar, why would I agree to hole up in this house for the rest of my life?"

"You understand what the job was about, right?"

"Taking care of all this junk!"

"It's not junk!" he said, getting testy. "It's history, it's meaning, it's life itself."

"Do all these junky things really matter so much?"

"Of course, they do. Yoli, your mother and father remember their wedding day every time they look at their wedding rings. They remember the first time you walked with that pair of bronzed *zapatitos* they keep on the mantel. You remember your high school graduation with the class yearbook. Mementos, objects, artifacts . . . I'm offering you the job of preserving memories. That's what all of these objects are. Not just a room full of wedding rings or teddy bears or wallets. They're rooms full of memories, the things that fortify and give meaning to our lives. This is the place where lost objects reside and are preserved for our memories."

"So this caretaker job is preserving memories, returning lost objects when the time is right and otherwise keeping them here," I said, putting it all together.

"That's right," Baldemar replied. "These objects have a purpose to fulfill, a job to do, and if their purpose hasn't been fulfilled, you need to return them to their owner so they can finish their job."

"And how exactly do I do that?"

He showed me the shoe box. Inside, amid all the tags was a pair of horn-rimmed eye glasses. He slowly took the labels off the glasses. As soon as he had, the glasses disappeared before my eyes!

"Once you take the tags off, the object returns to its rightful owner," he said. "Poof, returned to its rightful owner!"

I looked in the box. The glasses were indeed gone.

"So why don't you just take the tags off of everything and be done with it?" I asked.

"Chaos. That's what would happen. It's about knowing what objects haven't fulfilled their purpose and need to be returned, and which ones need to be kept here."

"Why would anything need to be kept here?"

"Would you return a gun or a knife to its owner if it meant in a drunken stupor he'd accidentally kill someone with it? Would you return a baby's toy if you knew that the child would later choke on it? The job comes with a lot of responsibility. And some objects, of course, need to be destroyed."

"The incinerator room."

"Exactly."

"And why is that?"

"Sometimes it's necessary to forget things," Old Man Baldemar replied. "No, let me rephrase that. Sometimes it is *imperative* that we forget things. Besides, this old house needs room for new lost items."

He saw that I was giving the whole matter a lot of thought.

"And there's the perk—immortality. I thought you were the one who could do that. Yolanda, I trust your judgment. I honestly thought you were the next caretaker. I guess I was wrong."

Oh, great, now he was going to guilt trip me! Truth was, now that the job was explained to me, it did have a certain appeal. Maybe this was what I was really destined to do with my life. But if not, what could it hurt to take on the job for a short time? At least until I figured out the art career thing. What did I have to lose?

"What if I take the job for a year," I offered.

"Nope," he said quickly. "Once you take the job, it's permanent."

"Permanent? What happens when I get sick or get old and stuff?"

"You won't get sick, ever. And you will not get old. It's that kind of job."

"Right, immortality." I said.

Geez, did I want to live forever?

"But I see that you've made your decision," the old timer said. "No matter what, right?"

I thought of my career in art and how I was going to work for it, no matter what! I had a choice here. And I was going to make that choice matter.

"That's right, Mr. Baldemar. I'll be an artist or die trying."

"Wait here," he said with a sigh.

He got up and shuffled down the hallway. I looked after him as he turned the corner and went down the adjacent hallway. I could hear him opening a door and walking into one of the many rooms. When he returned, I wondered what door he had opened. And why?

"Here," he said, and handed me a postmarked envelope. Of course! He must have gone into the room of lost mail.

The envelope was addressed to me! I read the return address: Parson School of Design. Oh my God! I quickly ripped open the envelope. My heart was pounding. My eyes could barely register the words on the page. "Dear Ms. Mendoza, it is our pleasure to inform you that you have been accepted as a Freshman to the Fall semester at the Parson School of Design."

I had made it to Parson! I felt the tears begin to flow. I turned to Old Man Baldemar.

"Oh, thank you! Thank you!" I said.

I turned and started for the door to tell my family, to tell the world! But the old man did something he had never done before. Before I could leave, he grabbed my arm and held me for moment.

"Yolanda, I gave you that letter so you could make an informed decision. You're certain this is what you want? The offer is still open. But the decision you make now is irrevocable."

That stopped me. "Irrevocable?"

This *was* an irrevocable life decision. Once made, for better or worse, it was what I would be doing. Manage memories, save lives, live forever or pursue my art, at best a risky proposition? Was I being selfish for wanting to pursue my dream? Maybe I *should* reconsider this.

Old Man Baldemar let go of my arm. "Sure you don't want to talk about this a little more?"

To my surprise I heard myself say, "Sure, let's talk some more."

LOST AND FOUND

The little girl. Six years old, maybe seven tops. Skinny legs, skinny arms, golden blonde hair. Big eyes. The eyes sucked me in—looking up at me. Pleading eyes, scared eyes. "Sir," she says. I can see she's pumping herself up, something she has to do but is not sure how to do it. But she gets it out.

"Sir. My parents just disappeared."

She looks around embarrassed. Looks at the other kids walking by with their parents, getting aboard the tram that goes over the causeway bridge to the new It's A Crazy World expansion. Just opened this morning and it's huge. The Psychodelic Roller Coaster ride, the Dr. Jekyll and Mr. Hyde Madhouse, Sybil's Merry Madness ride and so many more. They say this makes our park the biggest park in the world, bigger than the mouse and bigger than the gorilla. Unprecedented. You can't do it all in a week much less a day. Sections still under construction, expansion so big—rumor has it—that no one has a complete set of blueprints. The park now has its own zip code.

She looks enviously at the kids on their way to the Dementia Big Ride, walking with their parents, to the main promenade, to new shops and restaurants, to all you can eat, to the thrills a minute, to the scariest ride ever, to the security of a hug from mom, the safety of a ride home.

"Can you help me?"

Of course I can. We got protocol, rules, procedures. I follow them.

"My name is Choo-Choo Torres, what's your name?"

"Megan, Megan Tingle."

"Well, Megan Tingle, we need to tell people that your parents are lost. We need to ride in my go-cart, okay?"

She nods yes. I drive her in my beat-up trash slogger over to Communications Central and Randy Colson.

Randy's a couple of years older than me and really smart. Wants to do computer animation when he grows up—he's all into CGI and virtual imaging. So of course we hit if off from day one. The Park gets it that Randy is brain power and puts him in charge of all the surveillance computers at Communications Central. Yeah, I get a lot shit from him about how at least he's not emptying Crazy World trash cans.

Randy's in the surveillance office, his domain, sitting at a computer surrounded by dozens of mini-monitor screens showing security cams throughout the park. I explain to Randy the situation.

"Found her over by the tram station. No reports in yet?"

"Nope."

He looks the kid over. Those big eyes grab him too. "Parents probably lost track of her," he tells me.

"Yeah," I counter, "but wouldn't they check in with the Park? I mean, all-points bulletin or something? File a report?"

"It takes time. You can leave her here. I'll call the Park social worker."

Yeah, he'll take over. Find her folks in no time, I tell myself.

"Goodbye, Megan. This gentleman is going to find your parents for you."

"Thank you, Mr. Choo Choo."

Back to emptying the trash cans on the causeway bridge to Crazy World. Styrofoam boxes, cups, wrappers and all the unfinished food you'd ever want to see. This is what I do three days a week—Friday, Saturday and Sunday and, when I can. I even skip a class or two during the week.

I didn't get a full scholarship to USC, so I've got to make ends meet. And working at the Park, with its movie tie-ins makes a lot of sense. And makes money. Trojan cinema is not cheap. Film production major is monster expensive, even using the school's equipment. I planned to film my senior thesis film back in Arroyo Grande. But I got lots of static from the head of the department.

"Mr. Torres," he told me, "you know we insist on a team effort for the senior thesis."

"Yes," I replied. "I know that. I've gotten three classmates who have agreed to travel to Texas for a three-day shoot." I didn't tell him that Todd, Isaac and Mary Beth just wanted to get out of LA and Texas sounded like a fun adventure. I would be the writer/director, they'd be my producer, videographer and soundwoman. My crew fell in love with my screenplay. *Attack of the Lowrider Zombies*. It takes place in East Los Angeles. We'd shoot the establishing shots at the Evergreen cemetery—the zombie parts. Wide shots of the rampage down First Street, the attack on the Fourth Street bridge.

"But you're story takes place here in Los Angeles. Why do you need to go to Texas?"

How could I explain Max Martínez? The Maldonado Brothers, Junior Valdez, Bobby Hernández, Don Sebastiano—all the folks I wanted in the film playing themselves. I wanted to open it with a drooling Mrs. Romero zombie going after punky Reymundo Salazar. Hell, Arroyo Grande *is* East Los Angeles.

I corrected him, "Attack of the Lowrider Zombies takes place in *East* Los Angeles."

"East, West, it's still Los Angeles. I ask again why shoot in Texas?"

"It's the budget," I explained. "Yes, we'll shoot establishing shots in East Los Angeles but the interiors, the cemetery dialog scenes, the huge zombie crowd scenes—that's gotta be Texas. Non-union actors and everyone eager to work on a film for dirt little money. And I can pull in favors from old friends—locations, transpo, catering, all that will be free."

Finally Mr. Film Department Uberlord caved in. "Very well. We'll grant it. You're very convincing, Mr. Torres. That's a good trait for a filmmaker."

Duh.

So my mind's one hundred percent on the film.

Well, not exactly. The one thing I've been trying *not* to think about for the past few weeks is Yoli Mendoza, who is three thousand miles away at Parsons School of Design in the big *manzana.* And me here in LA wondering who she's with now.

Okay, the first few weeks apart were tough. I was lonely here in LA, and she was lonely in New York. Our lives together in Arroyo Grande were the glue that kept us talking on the phone every night. How's it going at USC? How're you doing at Parsons? Soon it was down to a call once a month. If I was lucky.

The first summer back in Arroyo Grande I knew something had changed. I took her out, a date just like the old days. I was so excited to see her again. Turned into a terrible night; ended with a huge fight. The usual—why my career was more important than hers. Me getting all defensive and hot tempered. It ended with me dropping her off at her house and Yoli running out of the car crying. Damn it, this is not what I wanted!

We saw each other a few more times during the summer, but it was always the same. She'd wind up crying or I'd wind up saying stupid things. At the end of that first summer, Yoli saw me off at the El Paso airport the second time, and we made a pact. We knew that the next three years of school would be difficult enough for us and that we didn't need any additional drama. So we agreed that we would not pressure each other during the next three years of college. No cell calls or texting—we'd leave each other alone. We were free to go out with whomever we wanted. After we graduated, if we both made it through college, we'd decide about us. We'd see then where we stood. Mature, realistic, adult reasoning.

And total bullshit.

Yeah, I don't know how I swallowed that one. But I did.

And I've played by the rules. I stopped pestering her. Now at the end of my senior year at USC, we talk once a month, if that. It's always my meager dime. And I can tell she's gotten on with someone else already. I hear her almost mention his name and then catch herself. Instead of "boyfriend and I went out to dinner in the East Village," it comes out. "I . . . was at this great restaurant in the East Village last night." Yeah, I'm not dumb. I know what the hell is going on. But those are the rules, and I agreed. But boy do I miss her. She's so much a part of me. How am I going to get through this? I'm afraid of what will happen when we graduate next month and meet to discuss our future.

Then it suddenly hits me. The reason I can't get the little girl out of my mind. Her eyes. Megan's got eyes just like Yoli Mendoza! Except for her blond hair, Megan is a dead ringer for Yoli when she was seven!

* * *

The next morning, Saturday, I arrive at the Park early and make my way immediately to Communications Central. I want to find out if they've reunited Megan with her parents. But when I get there, oh shit, what a commotion! Police. Lots of them. And men in suits, men who work out, men with grim faces, men with holsters under their jackets. I pull Randy aside. "What the hell?"

"The little girl. We couldn't find Megan's parents anywhere in the park."

"Whaaat?"

"We got surveillance showing the little girl with her parents boarding the tram and going into the new expansion, and we have surveillance of her walking by herself back across the bridge from Crazy World. We got her talking to you. But the parents never came back. I've gone through every surveillance camera we got and no sign of the parents. We're still searching in the new expansion. But it's so huge . . . and they never finished putting up all the surveillance cams in the undeveloped parts of Crazy World."

Eerie stuff, I'm thinking. Really weird.

"That's not all. Her parents are not the only ones."

"Huh?"

"Since the new expansion opened yesterday, we've gotten reports of nine missing people. Their friends or relatives claim they came to the park with them and that they just disappeared. Haven't shown up at home, tried calling them on their cells, nothing. PR is trying to keep a lid on it, but I don't know how long they can keep this secret."

"So that's all these cops, then?"

"And FBI, check it out!" He motions to a group of suited men conferring with Park engineers over a bundle of blueprints of the Park.

A helicopter appears overhead and a suit confers with the helicopter pilot over a walkie. Park managers are looking really scared and nodding their heads yes to everything that's asked of them. Yeah, a crazy world it is.

"Check this, Choo Choo," Randy says. He shows me a blow-up map of the park's Crazy World expansion. Randy's circled, in red, the places where people were reported missing. Eleven in all, counting Megan's mom and dad.

"All went missing within a one-mile radius of the Dr. Freud Performance Pavilion. Geez, I feel sorry for that little girl. You know what she asked me when I handed her over to Social Services? She said, 'Mr., are my parents dead?'"

As I leave Randy, I take one last look at the spots circled on the map.

* * *

I spend the morning on the causeway bridge. That's my assignment. Empty the ever-filling trash cans. This is America today—you demand what you want, eat what you want, trash what you want. And then leave it . . . someone else will take care of it for you. Really.

That someone else, of course, is me.

It takes about an hour for the trash bins to fill up—lots of drink empties, wrappers, half-finished this and partially eaten that. I load up the go-cart with stuffed plastic bags and then dump them in the trash bins behind the parking structure. Come back an hour or so later and the bins are full again. Twenty bins along the long arching causeway bridge to Crazy World. All the time I'm working this morning, however, I'm thinking of little Megan and her Yoli Mendoza eyes. "My parents just disappeared!"

Around noon, I see the park police questioning a man coming across the causeway from Crazy Land. He looks disoriented, confused and pissed off. I mean really agitated. I figure, this is too good to miss. I park the trash slogger by a nearby trash bin so I can hear the mayhem as I pretend to load up the trash.

"I'm not crazy!" he yells. "I'm telling you I came here this morning with my wife and two kids—boys, age seven and ten. I had to go to the john and when I came out, they were gone. They said they'd wait for me, but they were gone. I called my wife's cell. She keeps it in her pocket on vibrate when we come to the park because of this noise.

"But there was no answer. She *always* answers when I call! I wandered around a bit looking for them. Over there in the new rides area. I'm there maybe an hour, hour and a half. And then I walked back here and you're telling me its three days later?"

"It is Sunday, sir. That's a fact."

"We came here four maybe five hours ago, and it was Friday morning. For the opening of the Crazy World expansion! It can't be Sunday! That was just a few hours ago!"

"Sir, please come with us. We have surveillance footage of the park and I'm sure we can help you locate your family."

They walk him away. Last thing I see, he's shaking his head and shouting, "It can't be Sunday!"

Goosebumps for me.

The rest of the afternoon, in between emptying trash bins, all I can think about is how to find Megan's parents—where can they be? I imagine a worst-case scenario. What if Megan's parents *are* dead? What if we have a serial killer loose in the park? Maybe he's hidden the bodies of the missing people in some out-of-the-way dumpster or abandoned basement?

Who better to find out but me?

I decide to take a walk after I clock out at five. The Park is still packed with people. I cross the causeway bridge into Crazy World and go directly to the Dr. Freud Pavilion—it's got an eighties rock band playing to an enthusiastic crowd of grey-hairs. I begin to walk in concentric circles from the pavilion, seeking out any place where a body might be hidden. I look into the back areas behind the rides and booths, where chain-link fences with "Under Construction" signs let you know that Crazy Land is still a work in progress.

My keys let me past the locked gates and "No Entry" signs. But after searching for more than an hour, I find nothing. I head out to Communications Central to check in with Randy, maybe Megan's folks have been found.

I get there and discover the place is swarming with camera crews and remote trucks, reporters descending on the park like hungry vultures, eager for a morsel of breaking news, a scrap of scandal, a nibble of liability, a bite of injury. I pass by an on-camera talking head telling her viewers that people have gone missing in the new expansion for the *past two days*.

"The park has hushed it up!" she declares with alarmed indignation. "What's more, not only has the new expansion never been properly mapped, but aerial footage shows vast areas of the park still undeveloped."

Yeah, tell me about it. I know all about the miles of bull-dozed earth, half-constructed buildings with no roofs, dirt roads to nowhere, idle tractors and earth movers—management's hiccup trying to figure out what to build next.

And now the talking head has Breaking News—a half dozen people have come out of the new expansion that were *never recorded going in!* Oh yes, this is going to be big. The field reporter turns it over to the anchor at home base for a roll-in of interviews with the bewildered park visitors. I watch the broadcast on the reporter's field monitor. Some claim they entered by the main gate but they can't be found in the surveillance videos. And some, who were discovered in the Park, claim they don't know how they got there. They say they've never been to the Park ever, in their lives.

Ever.

I finally track down Randy. He's alone in his surveillance office surrounded by his battery of video monitors and computer hard drives.

"Randy, what the hell is going on?"

"Choo-Choo, it just gets weirder and weirder!" He hands me a beer from the secret stash he keeps under his desk—warm, but it does the job. Tells me he's had his hands full all day showing park security, the local PD and the FBI the surveillance videos he monitors. But the cops and FBI have left for now.

"Let me show you something." He rewinds a digital recording of surveillance from the causeway. "Check out this guy. This was taken yesterday."

He shows me an overweight slob in baggy cut-offs and a Lakers T-shirt trailing behind a wife, calling at him over her shoulder, and three sorry-looking teenagers, all wearing their Dodger baseball caps on backwards.

"He's one of the missing?"

"No. He's one of the ones that came out this morning, confused as hell, claiming he doesn't have a wife and family. Says he's gay and came here with his boyfriend. He's been trying to find his lover boy all morning. Check this."

Randy slaps another surveillance video into the playback and fast forwards it. I can see he's taken notes and finds the exact time code he's looking for. "Now, here he is this morning, coming out of Crazy World. Watch this."

"Yeah?" I say, trying to figure out what I'm supposed to be looking at. Then I see it. It's the same guy, but he's not a slob anymore. Buff. Six-pack. Tight fitting T-shirt. Trim mustache. But the same unmistakable face!

"That's the same guy?"

"Of course," Randy says, excited, guzzling his beer. "Just look at his face. But he's changed. And it's not just his clothing. He lost weight, he's worked out. Look at those pecs. How can he do that overnight? And he claims he came out of the Park the same day he entered."

"What are the Park people saying?"

"Choo-Choo, I've been at this all day and they're scared, really scared. It's not just the potential liabilities. Like what happens if someone shows up dead. It's that no one really understands what the hell is going on!"

"Deep."

"They've done helicopter sweeps of the whole park," the Rand continues. "They've done systematic foot patrol searches. And nothing, nada, zilch. And what some of these confused people are saying . . . that's wacky too, Choo Choo. Honest to God! The Feds are interrogating a guy this morning, and he lets slip that George W. is now the head of Fox News! He really believes that Bush went from being President of the United States to running the Fox News network! And a woman goes hysterical when we mention that Michael Jackson is dead. She claims to have seen him perform a week ago!"

"Sounds really bizarro, all right."

"Bizarro, Choo-Choo? Check this, they've called in a string theory expert from Cal Tech to consult with the FBI!"

"Whaaat? Cal Tech?" I'm asking myself, what the hell is string theory?

"Yeah, and after spending the afternoon examining all the videos and talking to the people who say they can't find their loved ones, and the people we didn't know were here who just showed up, he makes an on-the record statement to a closed-door session with park officials, local cops and the Feds."

Randy's fingers go Mozart on the computer keyboard, and another video leaps onto the preview monitor.

"I recorded the meeting. They didn't know I had a hidden camera in the room, so keep this to yourself." Randy pauses, takes a swing of his beer, and then pushes the play button. "Here's what Mr. Cal Tech has to say about it."

The video shows a cramped conference room. Camera is a ceiling shot looking over the heads of perhaps a couple dozen suits and uniforms. Addressing them is a guy looking about thirty but doesn't look like the nerd I expected at all. Shit, he's handsome. Sharp cutting features, rugged hair, deep eyes. And dresses like out of an Armani ad.

But once he opens his mouth: a total nerd.

"I have conducted interviews with individuals who claim to have lost loved ones, as well as those people who appear confused about their immediate surroundings and environment. Based on these interviews and the surveillance footage I have seen, I would offer a possible scenario that would explain the anomaly that would account for all the data we have so far. But, I must warn you, this scenario takes a little getting used to. I suspect many of you will find what I'm about to tell you very difficult to accept. I underscore, this is just a possibility, but it does explain all the evidence at hand."

The guy on camera stops for a moment and clears his voice, as if he's going to tell us the biggest lie in history and hopes he can pull it off.

"It *is* possible that some sort of . . . *wormhole* has appeared somewhere in the Park's new expansion area. It is possible that this is a *drifting* wormhole. It moves from here to there in the Park. And when it encounters someone, that person gets sucked into the wormhole."

The guy is interrupted by a commotion in the audience behind the camera. People wanting to know what the hell a wormhole is. People arguing among themselves. Mr. Cal Tech motions for silence, and finally things settle down.

He continues his spiel.

"Wormhole. Yes. No, not a black hole. A black hole is a singularity, a concentrated mass exerting intense gravity that pulls everything, including light, into an infinite concentrated point. Nothing can get out. A wormhole is different. It's a rift in the space/time continuum that connects two different points in space, like a doorway from one point in space/time to another. Wormholes up to now have been theoretical, predicted by Einstein's Theory of Relativity."

"But this one is real?" someone asks.

"We're speculating that one exists. An unstable, drifting wormhole. Imagine the spout of a tornado touching down here and there in the Park. Touching down just for a moment or two and not too big, but big enough to capture a person here and there. And once inside the wormhole, the person is sucked into some other place."

Randy gives me a "Can you believe this shit" look. This time I'm the one that takes a swig of beer. There is a clamor of voices in the audience as someone else asks a question.

"If this drifting wormhole exists, then where do all of these people go? And why only people, wouldn't other objects be sucked in?"

"Other objects . . . " Cal Tech responds, "that doesn't appear to be the case. It's just people. We don't know why. And we're thinking they probably go into some kind of other dimension. Possibly a parallel universe of some kind."

"What about the people who are coming out of the new expansion, the ones surveillance doesn't show ever going in?"

"The drifting wormhole would explain that as well. If it *is* a parallel universe connected to the other side of that wormhole, then we think people on the other side are walking into the other end of the wormhole in that universe and reappearing here in our own. So, John Doe walks into the wormhole here and disappears. A different John Doe, living in a different universe, walks into the other end of the wormhole in his world and reappears here."

Someone in the group asks a question, but the sound is bad and you can't make it out. But Mr. Cal Tech has heard it.

"Yes, exactly, we mistake the John Doe from the other universe for the guy that is missing here. But he may be a slightly different John Doe or maybe that John Doe doesn't exist in the particular parallel universe the wormhole has tapped into. That would explain why some people disappear and don't come back and some people appear who were never in the park in our universe. Remember, we are speculating an unstable wormhole. The other end taps into many different universes. That would also explain the time differential, why a John Doe may return to our universe hours or days after his counterpart has been whisked away from our end of the wormhole."

Randy turns off the monitor.

"Pretty weird shit, eh?"

"So what do all the honchos have to say? Did they buy into this?"

"The idea is so nutty no one wants to be the first to commit. The Feds, the local PD and the Park authorities are all wait and see. Even Mr. Cal Tech has qualifiers. He says if it is a wormhole, you'd expect to see all kinds of magnetic and gravitational disruption here on Earth. But so far they've not detected anything."

"And in the meantime people are still disappearing?"

"Three more reported today."

* * *

The metro ride from USC to Anaheim the next day is interminable. But I've got a game plan. I'll finish out my search of the one-mile area where people have gone missing. If I don't find anything, then I'll start searching the undeveloped back lot areas. I know I can find Megan's parents. And every time I think of Megan, I think of Yoli in New York.

When the metro finally arrives at the Park station, I get off and walk to the main Park entrance, where I get the surprise of my life.

The Park is closed!

Signs all over the parking lots and entrances declare the Park is temporarily closed for remodeling. Other signs instruct employees, that would be me, to report to Communications Central.

You gotta be kidding me!

Hundreds of Park employees stand around in front of Communications Central for an hour before the Director of Operations (we call him Major Dumb-oh) comes out to address us.

After a much rehearsed speech peppered with "until this mystery is solved" and "nothing to get alarmed about," Major Dumb-Oh tells us we're to finish our shift day and then get all our belongings from the lockers and clear the Park. "We'll be calling you all when we're ready to open the Park again."

My fellow bewildered and pissed-off employees begin to disperse, and I head out to the causeway bridge but decide to stop in on Randy on my way. I find him looking like forty miles of bad road. Did he even sleep last night?

"Choo-Choo," says Randy, relieved and brightening at my arrival. "Shit is crazier and crazier by the day."

"You telling me? They just closed the damn Park."

"Cover story is emergency remodeling repairs. Truth is they don't want any more visitors disappearing."

"You okay, Randy?"

"I'm really tired, was up all night. But listen to this. The powers-that-be had another closed-door session with the Cal Tech guy late last night. Once again, they didn't know I was recording it."

He leans across his cluttered table and punches a button on the preview monitor. The playback shows that high camera angle looking down at the backs of the suits and uniforms, but it's a smaller group this time, only about a dozen people. Mr. Cal Tech, with several other nerdy-looking guys, is in front of the group. Everyone looks deadly serious. One of the suits, obviously the Alpha Dog, is speaking.

"If this drifting wormhole theory is right, there may be other implications. I've asked Dr. Herbert Siegel from Cal-Tech to explain. Dr. Siegel?"

The Armani scientist I saw earlier addresses the group. No smiles and laughter this time. Now the guy is deadly serious. "My colleagues and I have been theorizing about the anomaly. And a question occurs. If there is an unstable space/time hole out there that floats about, why now and why is it limited to the new Crazy World expansion in the park?"

The bozos in suits look at each other. Each with a "Hey, I was thinking about that myself" look.

Cal Tech continues. "Could it be that this drifting wormhole has always been there? Perhaps not as intense or operative as now, but more subtly always there? We're wondering if some kind of space/time wormhole isn't just the natural order of things. Perhaps we're just noticing it now because of some enhanced crisis in the space/time fold."

A question from one of the suits. "Then why haven't we noticed it before?"

"Well, we considered that. And, after much discussion . . . " Cal Tech looks to his nerdy friends as if asking for permission. They nod for him to continue.

" . . . We're speculating that perhaps *we have noticed it before*. Perhaps we have noticed its effects before, but we've called it something else."

Silence. The suits all look at each other. And I'm thinking what they all must be thinking. Something else? What the hell is he getting at?

"Consider the experience of the people we've interviewed," Cal Tech goes on. "Each person still believes themselves to be the same person, even if, to our eyes, they may be somewhat changed. Here's what we think is happening. John Doe in this universe walks into the wormhole and reappears in a parallel universe ever so slightly different than this one. But John Doe still thinks himself or herself as the same person. They've not experienced any jolt, or passed out, no alarms have gone off. He or she may not even feel they are in a new place. To that person nothing appears to have changed. And when they do encounter differences in the world around them—because they *are* in a different universe—well, they just simply interpret these changes as a problem with their own perception.

"Perception?" someone asks.

"You walk into a room where you've been before in your old universe, but you haven't been there in the new universe, and yet it looks familiar. So you explain it away as *deja vu*.

Randy is nodding his head furiously, a goofy grin on his face. I notice he's half-way through another six-pack.

"In the old universe," Cal Tech goes on, "you paid your electricity bill this morning, but in this new universe you haven't yet, so when you notice this fact, you chalk it up to a slip of the mind. 'I thought I'd done that already.' In the old universe that neighbor's dog was named Rover; in this universe his name is Prince. You tell yourself, 'why can't I seem to remember that damn dog's name!' To all of these you think, 'My mind is playing tricks with me.' Because what's before you is obviously very real and tangible. And the memory you have of what was before is alterable. Your mind accepts your previous perception as a memory lapse."

The Alpha questioner is relentless. "But those are all minor instances. What about if you land in a universe where you're not married but in this one you are, or you don't have a sister in this universe but in the next one you do. How do you explain that?"

"Insanity, dementia, brain damage," Cal Tech responds without missing a beat.

"What we're suggesting," he continues, "is that our universe may be full of *many* drifting wormholes. And the portal to an alternate universe may be so subtle that we don't even notice when we've crossed into another alternate world!"

Wow! Well that does it for me! Thank you, Randy, thank you, Mr. Cal-Tech, thank all you weirdos who have nothing better to do than to make up bizarre theories of what my life, and the world, is about.

I want to get back to the Crazy World and its back lots, find Megan's parents and disprove all this wormhole hocus-pocus. But Randy wants me to stay, to talk about the Cal Tech guy's theories. Oh yes, by now Randy has a lot of theories of his own! He really likes the idea that, in fact, we've always lived in a world of drifting wormholes and that what is happening at the Park is just an extreme case of wormhole overload. "Wormhole overload?" Yeah, he actually said that.

* * *

I begin my final clean-out of the trash bins on the causeway bridge to Crazy Land and I start thinking about how I wish the Cal Tech guy's theory was real. That would mean that somewhere there is a universe where Yoli and I had actually gotten married at the end of our high school graduation, the way Mrs. Romero had predicted and we had planned it. And in that universe, Yoli is here with me in Los Angeles and not three thousand miles away in New York dating who knows who and making my life here miserable.

I'm wishing this not just because of what Mr. Cal Tech said, but because of the letter I got from Yoli yesterday. It's been weeks since I last heard from her and now, out of the clear blue, because of our pact, not a phone call but a *handwritten* letter from her. Is she ready to talk sense? To come out and join me in LA?

No.

"Dear Choo-Choo," the letter read, "I am writing to let you know some really great news! I have been accepted by the Sasonz Gallery for a one-woman show at the end of this summer! All my friends are jealous as hell. And you know how I got the show? I showed off the drawing I did of YOU to Mrs. Sasonz herself. Remember? The one of you at the Skyscraper pool when we were trying to figure out a name for that guy with no name? I had shown Mrs. Sasonz all of my other drawings and I thought she was ho-hum about it, but then she saw that drawing of you and said, 'This is real quality!' Anyway, I am writing to tell you I won't be coming home to Arroyo Grande this summer. I'm staying in New York to prepare the show. I'm sorry to disappoint you but I know you'll understand. My first one-woman show, wish me luck! Yoli"

Well, the damn letter made me cry. Of course! I sat in my dorm room and reread the letter several times and just cried my eyes out. I really, really missed her. And now I wouldn't be seeing her this summer after all! All I could think about was that she was gone from me forever.

* * *

It doesn't take me long to finish the trash dumping, and soon I am back in a now very empty Crazy Land expansion. I continue my search, but this time I am walking in the back lot area, behind the camouflaged barbed wire fencing that hides dirt roads leading to open fields littered with heavy dirt-moving equipment and stacks of building supplies—I-beams and stacks of lumber. As I look out at the vast expanse in front of me, I realize how daunting this search really is. If Megan's parents have been killed and buried here, it will take an army of search dogs and diggers to ever find them.

Another thought crosses my mind. All this time I've been hunting for Megan's parents I've been within that one-mile radius where everyone has disappeared. If this drifting wormhole does exists, I bet Park employees are probably not immune to being whisked away. I get creeped out.

And then I hear it. Two distinct voices, one male and one female, calling out from behind the battery of parked tractors, earth haulers and trucks.

"Megan! Megan!"

I run to where the vehicles are parked and arrive just as a haggard-looking man in shorts and a sweaty Hawaiian shirt and a women in cut-offs and cotton blouse come walking from behind the vehicles.

"Are you Megan's parents?" I shout, realizing just then how tense I feel.

"Yes!" The man replies, getting excited. "Do you know where she's at? We lost sight of her about an hour ago and have been looking for her all over this damn Crazy World complex."

"We've found your daughter," I tell him. "She's fine. Come along. I'll lead you back to the Park's Security Center. There's some people there who'll want to talk to you."

The rest is by the book. I transport the parents over to Park Security Center—they can't understand where all the crowds went who, by their account, were in the park only an hour ago. At Security the Park police are all over them with questions. I leave when they break the news to Mr. And Mrs. Tingle that they've been missing for three days. I don't get to see the reunion of Megan with her folks, but I'm happy to have helped make it happen. After I drop off the Tingles, I realize that in the commotion of finding them I've left my backpack at the Freud Pavilion. I return to the Pavilion, get my backpack and head out to Communications Central to tell Randy the good news. As usual, I find him hunkered down in the surveillance office, his hands flying over the computer controls of the surveillance cameras.

"Randy, I found the parents!" I tell him.

"Good for you, Choo Choo!" he says without looking up from the surveillance monitors.

"Hey," he continues, "that little boy's parents aren't the only ones who have been found. Look at this!" He points to several monitors showing people walking through the empty streets of Crazy World toward the park entrance. They look dazed and confused.

"With you finding Bobby's parents, that makes seven of the missing people who have turned up in the last two hours! How about that, Choo Choo?!"

"Randy," I reply, "it was Megan's parents I found. Hey, any word on when they'll be opening up the Park for business again?"

Randy drops what he's doing and turns around slowly to face me. He has a real strange look on his face.

"Choo Choo," Randy says, "what are you talking about? Who's Megan? You do mean Bobby's parents, right? The one's you've been obsessed with finding for the past three days? The Tingles?"

"Huh?" I reply. I'm suddenly feeling very confused.

"The parents of the kid you brought in from the causeway bridge three days ago. The kid with the big sad eyes, the first disappearance, Bobby Tingle?" He rifles through his desk and comes up with a photo of a seven-year-old boy.

"This kid here. It's his parents you just found, right?"

It takes a moment for it to sink in. I examine the photo, the face does look familiar. Then I realize Randy's right. Yes, of course! That's right, I remember now. It was a boy, not a little girl. And his name *was* Bobby . . . *is* Bobby. And I remember those eyes. Right, those pleading eyes, scared eyes. Megan? Where the hell did that come from?

A TEX-MEX NIGHT IN CHELSEA

"What kind of art does he do?" Jeannie de la Cruz wanted to know as we walked along 22nd Street, a sidewalk cluttered for blocks with the canvases of struggling artists who populated New York's Chelsea district. After picking Jeannie up at La Guardia, the taxi had dropped us off at 22nd and 8th Avenue, and we were on our way to meet my boyfriend of six months, Tommy, who had set up a display of his latest works outside the newly refurbished Chelsea Museum of Art.

"You'll soon see. It's kind of post-Warhol," I replied. "You know, finding beauty in the commonplace items of a consumer society. Tommy goes one step further: what he does is miniaturize the commonplace of old, denying its value. Like corporate logos—he repaints them and miniaturizes them on CD covers and such. You'll see. . . ."

"Sounds mighty, mighty exciting," Jeannie said, "and boy do I have a lot to fill you in on! I got the Fullbright I applied for! I'm going to do graduate research in Mexico."

"Oh great! Good for you!"

"I leave in a month to study under Dr. Armendáriz, the foremost expert on Mexico's pre-Columbian civilizations. I'll be involved in a new dig at the Templo Mayor, the main Aztec temple in Mexico City."

"With all that on your mind, I'm so glad you came out for the opening!"

"Yoli, I wouldn't miss it for the world!"

The opening was set for the end of the week and I was dying to show her the big discovery that I knew would put me on the art world map as soon as it was revealed. For weeks I had been reworking my portrait of Mrs. Romero, which was to be the *piece de resistance* of my one-woman show, and I wanted Jeannie, my *homegirl* from Arroyo Grande, to be the first to see it. I hadn't even shown my finished work to my heartthrob, Tommy, although I had hinted to him that he was in for a real surprise.

As we hurried along 22nd Street, I remembered again how much I loved Chelsea. The aged brownstone walk-ups, the refurbished warehouse spaces, bustling cafés with ancient brick storefronts, trendy outdoor restaurants and, of course, the countless, cruelly competitive, self-absorbed, recklessly self-aggrandizing but oh-so-chic art galleries. The scene was so different from Calle Dos in Arroyo Grande, where I had grown up and, yet, so perfectly suitable for my tastes now. Before long, we had to slow our walk because of the crowds taking in the array of sidewalk art on display.

"Boy, this place is mighty, mighty popular, huh?" Jeannie said.

"You ain't kidding," I said, jostling my way through the throng of humanity slowly inching its way down the sidewalk. "It's become the Mecca of the art world."

"Yoli, I can't believe that guy is selling this painting for only $10?" Jeanie said, pointing to large oil canvases, some five- or six-feet square, that lined the sidewalk next to a large sign that read: "Own a Reichenbach. Pay what you think it is worth—nothing over $10."

"Good afternoon, Yoli," the man hawking the large oils said as we passed by. The drab, worn jeans, faded flannel shirt and paint-splattered Yankees baseball cap, framed a beaming face with bushy white eyebrows, intense blue eyes and a handlebar mustache. "How's that special portrait coming?"

"Almost finished," I replied. "Going to unveil it at my one-woman show at Sazonz's at the end of the week."

"The Sazonz Gallery? Good for you! But remember, private and public. The two go hand in hand!"

"You'll come, won't you? I got a big surprise in store."

"Count me in!"

"Who was that?" Jeannie asked as we moved along. She looked over her shoulder at the old man's shabby appearance. "Poor guy sure looks down and out."

"Oh, that's Old Man Reichenbach himself. We've become friends."

"Reichenbach? . . . I've heard that name."

"Sam Reichenbach," I explained as we made our way past his mobile gallery. Reichenbach's works covered at least half the block between 8th and 9th Avenue on 22nd Street, dozens of large canvases leaning three and four deep against building walls. "He was big in the 60s, one of the founders of the American Pop movement. Was right up there with Andy Warhol, Roy Liechtenstein, Claes Oldenburg and James Rosenquist. Became a millionaire overnight."

"Well, he doesn't look much like a millionaire now."

"In 1980, he had a Road-to-Damascus type epiphany. He became disgusted with how the art market worked. In those days all he had to do was spit on a canvas, sign it and it would sell for thousands of dollars. But it could only be bought by rich art collectors or museums; common folk rarely got a chance to see his works. He decided that he had gotten away from why he had wanted to do art to begin with—to share his artistic vision with as many people as possible. So he became obsessed with the notion of *public art*, or as he puts it, "art for the people." He decided to do a one-man protest of the arbitrary nature of the art market. For years now he's been flooding the art market with his own works. He paints feverishly, cranking out dozens of these oils a week, and sells them all for less than $10."

"$10? That's pretty darn cheap."

"Yep, that way anybody can buy one. Public art!"

"But doesn't that bring down the value of his previous works?"

"Exactly what he wants to happen. The museums and rich collectors hate him. They've paid tens of thousands of dollars for his works—several have sold for over a million dollars each. Works that are identical to ones that he now sells for only ten bucks. To further confuse the issue, he's post-dated the new works so now no one knows which were painted before and which were painted after his epiphany."

"Wow," Jeannie said taking it all in. She stopped to admire a particularly beautiful abstract piece done in contrasting hues of deep reds, pale oranges and vibrant pinks. "So, how much are all these paintings really worth then?"

"No one really knows," I replied, taking in the piece Jeannie was ogling. Hey, Jeannie had taste, that I'll have to say. The red abstract was probably the best painting on exhibit.

"Appraisers all disagree. Some say a piece like this one may be worth as much as a half million dollars because it's a Reichenbach. Others say it's only worth what you paid for it as sidewalk art. The other sidewalk artists, of course, hate him, too. Don't mention Reichenbach to Tommy!"

"Hate him?" Jeannie asked, puzzled.

"Sure, he's had a devastating effect on the local sidewalk art scene . . . as you might well imagine. Why pay a hundred bucks for an oil by an unknown struggling artist when you can get a Reichenbach for only ten?"

"Say, maybe I should buy one."

"Sure," I replied. "I have a half dozen in the basement."

A few minutes later we arrived at the corner of 24th Street and 10th Avenue, Jeannie proudly lugging the red abstract that she'd admired—she'd gotten it from Reichenbach for only $7!

"That's him," I said as I pointed to where Tommy had set up the display of his work in front of the expanded Chelsea Museum of Modern Art. "He's the tall guy with the wavy hair."

"Yoli, he's a hunk," Jeannie said scrutinizing Tommy in a way that might have made me pretty damn jealous had Jeannie not confided to me, back in high school, that she was gay.

"Well?" Jeannie said turning to me in a way she hadn't done since those confidante days at Jefferson High. "So how is he? I mean, you know . . . ?"

"Jeannie, really!" I said surprised at her crassness.

"Yoli, the truth!" Jeannie pressed. She gave me that I-want-to-know-all-about-it look that I hadn't seen since she asked me how good a kisser Choo Choo Torres was after our sixth-grade graduation party.

"Okay, he's good . . . real good." I said with a certain degree of pride.

"I knew it!" Jeannie beamed. "Lucky girl!"

"Jeannie, I hate to say it but you can only spend so much time in bed. Anyway, our relationship is about more than just that."

"Oh," Jeannie said, delighting in getting to me. "*Our relationship is about much more than just that*," she repeated.

With that we both busted up. That's why I love Jeannie so much! It was at that moment that I realized how much I had missed her and her friendship since graduation. Oh yeah, there was that awkward moment in our senior year when she told me about her sexual orientation. But heck, we had been such good friends for so long that it didn't matter a bit. My response had been to give her a big smacker on her lips and then say, "Okay, you're gay. I'm not. With that behind us, can we continue to be the good friend we are!" And of course we became even closer after that.

"Tommy Bartel," I said, introducing Jeannie with a sweeping gesture, "this is my oldest and best friend from Arroyo Grande, Jeannie De La Cruz! Jeannie, this is my ever-loving Tommy Bartel."

Tommy and Jeannie awkwardly shook hands, then Tommy was called away by a tourist interested in buying one of his pieces. This allowed me time to explain Tommy's work to Jeannie.

"You see, a lot of pop artists look at the commonplace and draw attention to it, forcing us to look at it in a different way . . . as art. With Tommy, it's taking items like corporate company logos that have come to dominate our daily visual experience, and miniaturizing them. This denies their overpowering influence over us and allows us to expunge them from our lives by hanging them into a tiny corner of our home. In this way we are the ones who define their role in our lives, not the other way around."

"Right," Jeannie said.

I could see she was not entirely convinced. I looked across the way and saw that Tommy had made a sale. He came back to us, beaming.

"An NBC peacock logo, four inches by four inches, and it went for $300 bucks!" he said proudly.

"Great," I replied, "then maybe you can treat us to dinner tonight?"

"Oh gee, Yoli, I forgot to tell you. I've got to make a delivery to *Art Forum*. You know, for the piece they're running on me in the October issue. Why don't we get together tomorrow night. No wait, that's my *chiaroscuro* class—I have to make that. Well, let's try for the end-week after your opening. I promise, after the show I'll treat you both to dinner! I'll make it up to you, really!"

¡Híjole! To say I was disappointed would be an understatement. I had told Tommy all week long what a dear friend Jeannie was, and he had promised to join us for dinner. Now, he was begging off. But some part of me wasn't so surprised. Ever since he'd heard about my opening at the Sasonz, he'd been acting funny.

Six years older than me, he'd been trying for a one-man show in Chelsea since arriving in New York ten years ago—with no luck. And here I come, not a year out of Parsons and my senior thesis project propels me into a one-woman show at the most prestigious gallery in Chelsea. Nope, I wasn't all that surprised.

"Sure, Tommy" I said, trying to hide my disappointment. "We can do dinner after the reception."

"Yoli, I have another customer. Excuse me. Nice meeting you, Ginny." With that he was off to engage an elderly couple who were examining one of his miniature pieces.

"Ginny?" Jeannie said, obviously miffed.

"Sorry," I said, sucking it all up—he'd pay for this one.

"Look," I said, "Let's get us home and unload your bags."

I started out toward the subway. I could tell Jeannie was seeing through my bravado but was being cool about not making an issue of it. Damn it! Why did Tommy have to go and ruin everything?

* * *

"And this is my studio," I said proudly as I flicked on the light switch which illuminated the large second-story warehouse loft. I ushered Jeannie in and locked the door behind us, throwing the stack of mail onto the kitchen table.

"Just put your things over there." I motioned to the bed on the floor which, next to a rumpled couch, a table and chairs, was the only other furniture in my loft.

"This place is great! It's mighty, mighty roomy! My God, Yoli, look at all these paintings!" she said as she examined my workspace, where I had several easels up and dozens of oil portraits stacked in groups along the walls.

"Yoli, I can't believe it! Hey, here's Old Man Baldemar!"

I smiled. Jeannie had homed in on my Arroyo Grande series. I had spent all summer working on portraits of friends and acquaintances from my home town. It was part of what I would exhibit at the opening later in the week.

"Yoli," Jeannie asked, "what's he holding?"

"A letter," I replied, "don't ask."

"And here's Terri Butler, and Max Martínez . . . Junior Valdez . . . Yoli, these are wonderful!"

"Do you really like them? My thesis prof at Parson thought they were 'distinctive.' Said it's the best portraiture work she's seen in years."

"They're fabulous! Oh look, here's Doña Cuca Tanguma, those crazy glasses of hers—you captured it perfectly! And this must be Father Ronquillo, his sweaty headband, of course! Real good likeness. And Choo Choo! Oh my God, Yoli, have you heard from Choo Choo? What's going on with you guys?"

"Oh, we email each other now and then. I think he has a girlfriend."

"Still upset that you dropped him, eh?"

"Oh, I think he's over that—four years, please! He's all wrapped up in his filmmaking."

I could feel my eyes beginning to water up. Geez, thinking of Choo Choo still did this to me! I wiped away a tear and put on my best face. "Did I tell you his senior thesis film will be set in Arroyo Grande? I think he's shooting it this week."

"Really?"

"Yeah, it's a spoof on that old George Romero classic, *Night of the Living Dead*. Choo Choo calls it *Attack of the Lowrider Zombies*." I couldn't help it, I wiped away another tear.

"So, Yoli," Jeannie said, tactfully changing the subject, "How do you remember all these faces, and in such detail?"

"My notebook, remember?" I walked over to the table and picked up my bulging notepad of pencil and charcoal sketches that had come bubbling up from Mrs. Romero's sinkhole and that had started me on my career in art.

"See," I said, showing off some of the sketches in the book, "I sketched all these people back home years ago—here we all are at the Skyscraper that Flew. Now, I just work from my sketches."

"Awesome!"

"Jeannie, I can't wait any longer. I gotta show you something. You'll be the first person to see it. You ready for something really cool?"

"What can be cooler than all of these portraits?"

"You're not going to believe this. I mean this isn't just cool. It's . . . damn it, it's historic!"

"Historic?" Jeannie said with an aren't-you a-little-over-the-top look on her face.

"As you would say, 'mighty mighty' historic," I replied. "As a matter of fact, it will rewrite the laws of physics."

With that, I pulled her over to a corner where a large easel stood covered by a bed sheet. "All right, I want you to sit down here and, as Mrs. Romero would say, *prepárate!*" Jeannie sat down in front of the easel, as told, and I moved behind it.

"Are you ready?"

"Oh, come on, Yoli! Get on with it! Rewrite the laws of physics already!"

With that I lifted the sheet off the painting and watched as Jeannie reacted.

She was silent at first, taking in the painting, and then said, with a puzzled look, "Yoli, this is Mrs. Romero."

"Yes, it's Mrs. Romero."

"But there's something strange about this painting. Mighty, mighty, strange. It's really cool and all, but there's something *more*."

"Oh, *much* more, Jeannie."

"Oh, my God, Yoli, much, much more! What am I missing? Why is this so . . . Yoli, I've never seen anything like this before!"

"No one has, Jeannie." I said, trying for all I was worth not to blurt it out. "What do you suppose it is?"

"Her likeness is really true. I mean that is definitely Mrs. Romero. Waving at us the way she does from her front porch, and there's her dog, Junior, at her side."

"Yep, I took the image from one of my sketches. But there's something else, Jeannie. Can you see what it is?"

"Yes, oh, my God! Now I see it, Yoli. Oh my God, now I see it!" She stood up and went right up to the portrait. "This color . . . Yoli, this isn't blue, right? And it's not green, it's not gray. It's not red. And it's not orange. But it's so vibrant! It's . . . Yoli, *what color is this?* I don't think I've ever seen this color before!"

I beamed back at her, not saying a word.

"Yoli," she said really getting agitated, "*where* did you find this color? I mean I can't even find words to describe it!"

The more she examined the portrait of Mrs. Romero waving from her front porch, the more furrowed her brows became. "Yoli," she kept insisting, "I've never seen this color before, *in my entire life!*"

"That's right," I said triumphantly, "*no one* has never even seen this color before. Ever!"

"Huh?"

"Jeannie, the color you see before you, the color I used to paint Mrs. Romero's portrait, has never been used before. In fact, it's that very color that's going to put me on the art world map. Jeannie, *I've discovered a color that is not found in the known spectrum of light!*"

* * *

A few minutes later, after Jeanie's astonishment abated, I sat her at the kitchen table, where I had set up a triangular glass prism that caught the afternoon light through the open window.

"See, here is red and green and blue," I said, pointing to the array of light emanating from the prism. "But look, where can you find this color? You see, it's not any variation of any of these basic colors."

"I guess. I mean, it reminds you of blue, but not really. And it is kind of reddish, but not really. I mean there's nothing to compare it to. It's just so distinctive and different and . . . unique! How do you talk about a color that no one has ever seen before?"

"And not found on the light spectrum!"

"But how can that be? I mean, isn't color defined as what we see on the spectrum of light?"

"That's what they say, but that doesn't change what's in front of your own eyes."

I motioned for Jeannie to follow me to the window. "Come look."

I had set up another glass prism at the window, this one much larger. The prism cast the afternoon sunlight coming through the window into a multi-hued display on a piece of white poster board I had set up.

"See," I said, pointing to the board, "here's the full range of colors visible to the human eye from the color spectrum."

"And over here, not visible to the human eye, would be your ultraviolet." I pointed to the other end of the light display. "And over-here would be infrared, but our eyes can't detect that. But you can see this color should logically fit in here some place."

I pointed to the space between the red and blue color shift. "But it's not there. There is no visible color that our eyes can detect that is like the color of the paint I use. I think the paint *transforms the light that hits it*, and our eyes see this transformed light as a color we've never seen before."

"Yoli, this is amazing! I mean, it's not just an art thing. This is like an important scientific discovery. Like Newton's apple and Einstein's relativity. I mean, this could revolutionize the whole world, this could . . . " She suddenly understood what I had said earlier. " . . . *rewrite the laws of physics!*"

"Well," I said with feigned modesty, "I'd just settle for making a splash in the world of art."

"And you haven't shown this to anyone?"

"Just you. Not even Tommy, though I was going to show him tonight after dinner. That's what he gets for standing us up."

"Yoli," Jeannie said taking it all in, "how did you come up with this? What are you, a mighty, mighty scientific genius now?"

I walked over to my work table and picked up a tube of paint and handed it to her.

"Medium Xenosium," Jeannie read the inscription on the tube of paint.

"I looked it up. It comes from the Latin, 'xeno,' meaning 'foreign or stranger.'"

"Where'd you get this?"

It took only a beat, but the smile on my face, I guess, said it all. We said it in unison: "Mrs. Romero's sinkhole!"

I walked back to the painting. "Jeannie, what is the best thing about this painting?"

"Why, the color, of course!"

And, of course, that is exactly what I feared she would say.

* * *

"What do you mean, you can't go through with it?" Jeannie asked as she stuffed a mouthful of fettuccine Alfredo into her mouth.

We were seated in an outdoor café in the East Village, and I had been pouring my heart out to her about the biggest personal decision I had to face since telling Choo Choo that I couldn't marry him at the end of our senior year in high school.

"Well, *pensándolo bien*, I don't want to be a successful artist because of a gimmick!" I said, trying to be as concise and to the point as possible.

"What gimmick? The fact that you are using the coolest, unknown, amazing never-seen-before color in the history of human civilization has nothing to do with the fact that you are a great artist. Yoli, you've just graduated, and just look at your body of work! And you're showing at the coolest gallery in Chelsea."

"But look at what people are going to see," I said picking at my food. I had long ago lost my appetite. This was the one driving dilemma that had plagued me for weeks—ever since I had completed Mrs. Romero's portrait. But at least I now had someone to talk to about it.

"People are not going to see my talent as an artist. They're going to be overwhelmed by a color that no one in the history of the world has ever seen before. And *that* is how people will think of me. Not Yoli Mendoza, the great artist, but Yoli Mendoza, the girl who introduced 'xenosium' to the world!"

"No doubt about that."

I could tell she was hearing my soul.

"My one-woman show will be forgotten and my art work will be forgotten. Instead it'll be all about xenosium and its peculiar properties, and why wasn't this ever discovered before, and who patented it, and who produced the tube of paint, and what does the scientific community think of it, and how will it affect the art market and etcetera and etcetera. At best, I'll be remembered not because I'm a good artist—which I damn well am!—but because I was the artist that was lucky enough to accidentally find a tube of paint. A tube of paint no one's seen before! God knows where it came from or who invented it!"

Jeannie stopped eating. I guess I had really gone on a tirade and she could tell that I needed some back up.

"Yoli, you're absolutely, unquestionably, and absolutely dead right. As incredible as this xenosium is, I think you have to put it away."

"Put it away?" I asked anxiously.

In spite of all my agonizing, the idea of totally rejecting or denying xenosium hadn't ever entered my mind. My thought had been about how to circumvent xenosium, get the upper public relations hand on this, how to promote my art in spite of xenosium. But, *híjole*, here was Jeannie suggesting something totally radical: tossing this miraculous discovery out, entirely!

"Say that again," I asked wanting to make sure I had heard right.

"You said it yourself. As long as xenosium is around, your art work is not going to be taken seriously. And your work is mighty, mighty fine, so don't even show this xenosium piece. The reason you were selected for this one-woman show is not because of xenosium, but because you're an artistic genius—so show *that* off!"

I was silent for a long while, letting the insidiousness of it all sink in.

"Jeannie," I said slowly, trying to compose my words, "That would mean . . . "

"I know exactly what it would mean," she said. "And, as a friend and homegirl, I'm telling you that is exactly what you should do!"

* * *

The next several days passed by quickly. Once prodded into what I knew in my heart of hearts I should have done a long time ago, it was just a matter of budgeting my time to do all the necessary things that I had to before the Sasonz opening. I began, of course, by destroying the portrait of Mrs. Romero. Yes, it was a ghastly act, but once Jeannie had convinced me of what I had to do, I set about it with a determined passion. I recruited a reluctant Jeannie to help—after all, she had put me up to the deed!

"Oh Jeannie, this is so gross!" I said, slicing the canvas with a box cutter. "It's like killing Mrs. Romero herself!"

"She's already dead, remember? Just do it!" Jeannie commanded as she helped push the canvas pieces into the trash can. "Sometimes you have to destroy something you love in order for it to live again with more meaning."

"Well, *that* sounds like a crock of bullshit. Do you know this for a fact?"

"No, but we'll know it for a fact once we finish the deed!"

The next part was harder. Actually repainting the portrait of Mrs. Romero from my sketches, but without xenosium. I spent hours and hours trying to find the right color scheme. The truth of the matter was that xenosium *had* been ideal color for the portrait of Mrs. Romero. Now, every color I tried seemed forced, inadequate, aesthetically inappropriate . . . or just plain ugly!

I finally settled on an array of subtle greens for the background, taking a page from the portraiture of San Antonio artist César Martínez and then, for the highlights of Mrs. Romero face, utilizing vibrant reds and oranges, a nod to the feminist renderings of Ester Hernández. After I got over my initial nostalgia for xenosium, I realized that the results were not bad at all!

The more I looked at the colors and the likeness of Mrs. Romero (I do believe I rendered a better likeness this second time around), the more I began to really like the painting.

Since I had started on the new portrait, I hadn't checked my messages and was surprised to find that among the dozen of overlooked calls, there was a call from Tommy. Once again, I was not surprised to hear that he had been called away for an emergency meeting of the Chelsea Art Collective he chaired, and that he would not be able to attend my opening. I guess that's when I made up my mind about *him*!

* * *

"Jeannie! Hurry, hurry!"

We scrambled out of the taxi in front of the Sasonz Gallery, Jeannie paying the driver as I hurried into the main gallery dragging Mrs. Romero's portrait, carefully wrapped as the painting was still wet in a couple of places. Although we were more than an hour early, I could see that people were already gathering. I ushered myself into the gallery and went directly to Mrs. Sasonz, who was doing a last minute walk-through to the Arroyo Grande portraits along one side of the large exhibit hall.

"Yoli!" she blurted out, in a reprimanding tone. "This is not the proper way to deliver a work for a major show!" I could tell she was really stressed out because I was dragging in the main portrait of the show at the last hour. Off to the side I could see several officious-looking people sipping wine in the gallery antechamber.

"I'm so sorry, Mrs. Sasonz! I just had to add some finishing touches."

She softened, "Well, child, let's get on with hanging it so we can get on with the evening."

She walked me to the center of the exhibition hall where she had set up a pedestal for the portrait of Mrs. Romero. I'm glad I didn't know about this before, *it was so intimidating!*

I hurriedly unwrapped the portrait and showed it to Mrs. Sasonz.

She was transfixed.

"My God, Yoli, I had no idea."

She took a long walk around the painting, squinting now and then, back off and then coming in closer to examine details in the painting. Finally she spoke again.

"My God, this is magnificent! It's the best work I've seen of yours. This will put you on the map! And I know just the buyers who will bid for this one. That's what we're going to do, Yoli, make this painting the prize of a bidding war!

She turned to her assistant, "This will cover us for the rest of the year."

Just then I heard a voice behind me, a voice I hadn't heard for years. It was at once familiar and oddly strange, here in the Chelsea art district.

"Yoli . . . "

I turned and I found my hand covering my mouth as I let out a gasp.

My mind frantically raced as it registered what my eyes were telling me but my heart was also telling me could not be. Standing on the other side of the velvet stanchions of the gallery entrance was Choo Choo Torres!

"Sorry to surprise you," he said apologetically, "but you know I couldn't miss your first one-woman show!"

"Choo Choo!" Jeannie shouted as she caught sight of him. "You came!"

"Of course, I came! Broke my piggy bank, put off my film shoot for a few days, bought a ticket and flew out this morning. I wouldn't miss Yoli's big day for the world!"

I ran to him, wrapped my arms around him and found myself giving him the longest kiss I had ever given anyone in my life.

How could I not fall in love with Choo Choo all over again?

THE TESTAMENT OF OFFICER BOBBY HERNÁNDEZ

Okay, I'm making this videotape to get things off my chest. There are things that have been with me for three years now, terrible things that are eating away at me. At night I might be asleep and then, suddenly, I wake up and I think about what I saw that night and what it must mean, the implications. And then suddenly I'm wide awake. I can't get back to sleep. I sweat—that cold, clammy, non-stop sweat that makes your hair stand on edge and stains your underwear and leaves you exhausted.

At that point, I usually get up and walk around the house. My wife Bertha and I live in the small house behind my parents' home at 615 Calle Cinco in Arroyo Grande, Texas. That is, until Bertha left me.

The house reminds me always of the good times we used to have. We got married right after we graduated from high school. I was lucky to get in on a new training program offered by the Arroyo Grande Police Department—two years away at the police academy in Phoenix, Arizona, and then back to Arroyo Grande as Officer Robert Hernández.

Once I'm awake, I pace around in the living room, sweating and thinking about the terrible things I saw that night. I worry that I have never said anything about it, even after I quit being a cop. I had been on the Arroyo Grande police force for four years when it happened. I quit three years ago because of the nightmares and the night patrols that reminded me of that awful night. I couldn't take it anymore.

I know in my heart of hearts that I can't and won't ever say these things out loud to anyone. I've tried doing that several times and I know what happens, and what it does to me. That tightening feeling in my throat, my eyes burning, the ringing in my ears, my heart palpitations, the feeling that I am about to suffocate. The memory alone gives me the shakes . . . fear. That deep-sinking fear that the world is not as it should be and never again ever will be.

And then comes the drinking—a shot of whiskey first, just to settle my nerves, you know, just to ease me down, to help me forget. And then another. And then a beer chaser. And then more of the hard stuff. Anything to help make that memory go away. Just to settle my nerves, you see? And I drink, and I drink, and I drink. Eventually I pass out. And if I'm lucky, I don't have the nightmare.

This weekend, I decided to clean out the attic. I thought maybe that might take my mind off it. That's when I found that old video camera that Choo Choo Torres used to play with when we were kids. He gave it to me when he went off to USC.

"Use it to make your own movie," he said.

So I've set it up here in the living room. Ready to talk. I frame up on the empty chair, turn on the "record" button and then go sit in the chair facing the camera. This is Bobby Hernández, I say into the camera, and I'm going to talk about what happened that night in Arroyo Grande. So help me

God, this is what really happened. So help me God . . . if there still is one.

I stop for a moment and wait. Nothing happens. Okay, so far so good. Yeah, this is really good, just to get it off my chest! Here goes.

The day after I saw what I saw at the Ramírez house, I discovered that I could not speak about it. That morning I had come back to the station at the end of my shift, seven o'clock. I found Chief Tom Bowers in the station kitchen.

"Coffee?" he asked, indicating the carafe he was holding.

I nodded yes.

"Heard the city council passed that resolution last night," he said, pouring the coffee for both of us, "the one giving Rebber and Barrón the green light to destroy those condemned houses on Calle Cuatro. Once that Casino complex is built, this town's going to pop—recession or not."

"Uh-huh," I responded, trying to find the words to tell him what I saw.

"That'll mean more crime here in Arroyo Grande. We'll have to beef up the force," he says, and hands me my cup. "So how was the shift? Anything I should know about?"

It was a ritual with us. Usually I said nothing. If I was really talkative I might venture with, "Same 'ole, same 'ole" or "What does a night of patrolling Arroyo Grande and watching paint dry have in common?" You know, anything light, joking. Something to confirm to Chief Bowers that once again, like countless other nights, the gentle people of Arroyo Grande had slept their peaceful slumber without incident.

But this morning I had something to say, something terrible and alien, something sinister and dark, something that would shock those peaceful people out of their sweet dreams and send them screaming from their beds into the streets. If only they knew. But they didn't know. Only I knew and I had to tell someone.

But even as I opened my mouth to tell him that something terrible had occurred in Arroyo Grande, I suddenly found myself fighting some inner demon that had taken hold of my body. My throat tightened, the constriction causing me to gasp for air—I couldn't open my mouth! I was suffocating. Suddenly I found my eyes burning, a deep stinging pain that forced me to close them tightly. And then the deafening ringing in my ears, filling my head with a pain worse than any migraine I had ever experienced.

"Bobby? You okay?" Chief Bowers asked.

I could barely hear his words for the ringing in my head. I dropped the coffee cup and felt my legs give out from under me. As I started to fall, Bowers caught me and settled me into a nearby chair.

After a moment I was able to catch my breath. Then the ringing in my ears began to subside. "I think I'm okay now." I replied.

He gave me the once over while sipping his coffee.

I knew what he was thinking. I could see it in his eyes. *Bastard's fallen off the wagon again. I shouldn't have given him another chance*. I could see it in his eyes.

"Just tired," I quickly lied. "You know, a long night."

The chief put his coffee down and started out to his office. "Yeah, well, you best get home. You're off tomorrow, right?"

I nodded agreement, relieved that the burning in my eyes had stopped.

"Rest," he said as he left me. "Rest."

Later that evening, after I had gotten up from my afternoon nap and could smell Bertha's *guisado* wafting up from the kitchen below, I decided I really did have to tell someone about what had happened. I don't like to get Bertha involved in my work, but this was something out of the ordinary. I had to tell someone, and who better than my wife? So I went down to the kitchen.

"Bertha, *mi amor*," I began as I poured myself a cup of coffee, "the strangest thing happened last. . . . "

And then it began again, my eyes burning, the gasping for air, the ringing in my ears, my heart palpitating. The same damn thing happened again. That's when I knew I couldn't do it again—it was a warning. One that I knew I would obey.

After that, I no longer tried. It was as if Alfonso Ramírez had put some kind of hex on me, a spell, some *brujería.* I knew that I would have to hold this terrible secret of the Ramírez family inside me. I have now for three years. Until now. Maybe it's that I'm alone. Bertha left me a month ago, said she couldn't put up with my nightmares anymore. Said either I got some psychiatric help or she was leaving. She didn't understand it when I told her I couldn't talk to anyone about it, that Ramírez wouldn't let me.

"Bobby, the Ramírez family moved away three years ago," she said. "How can they stop you?" Then she went into the bedroom and packed her clothes in a suitcase, crying the whole time.

I don't blame her for leaving.

Yes, the Ramírezes are gone. But I also know their power is still here.

* * *

It started out as a pretty normal night. I had signed into the station and, after some small talk with Andy Armenta coming off the day shift, I grabbed my thermos of java and headed out the door. The routine was simple enough. Just cruise the town once, come back to the station, watch television until midnight, cruise the town again, return to the station and, on most nights, take a nap till six o'clock for the third and final patrol of the town and get back to the station by seven for the shift change.

On this night I pulled out of the station at Calle Uno and Sycamore and started out on my usual loop, which took me east to Interstate 10, making sure there were no stranded motorists, then getting back onto surface streets, heading down Pershing Street to Calle Diez. Then I'd swing around by the cemetery on the south side of town. Eventually, I'd find myself back at Calle Mercado. After years of patrolling Arroyo Grande, I had gotten used to checking out certain familiar places, places I had long ago determined would be logical places for someone to engage in mischief.

I was never disappointed. The back of the high school stadium was one of these sites, where once or twice a month I'd cough up teenagers sipping beer or smoking pot. The wide plaza in front of the Barrón and Rebber skyscraper was another, with its hidden nooks and crannies ideal for drug deals. And, of course, the grassy rise by the gates to the Arroyo Grande cemetery, a great place for some patron of the Copa de Oro to sleep off a *borrachera*.

Most of the time, the majority of the many, many nights I patrolled Arroyo Grande, nothing, absolutely nothing, happened. The gentle people of Arroyo Grande slept their peaceful sleep and gathered their strength for the many chores ahead of them the next day. This night was such a night, or so I thought. The first patrol was uneventful. I returned to the station and caught the evening news and the "Tonight Show," then, at midnight, I set out on the second patrol of the night. And that's when it all changed. I had just passed the cemetery and pulled onto Calle Mercado, when I saw the toddler.

Ordinarily, seeing a three-year-old riding his tricycle along the bumpy sidewalk of Mercado Street, negotiating the rise and fall of concrete where the roots of large oaks had undermined the sidewalk, would not draw my attention. But this time it did. At one o'clock in the morning, you can bet it did!

I slowed down the cruiser and pulled alongside the boy. Then I noticed who it was—Jimmy Ramírez, the youngest of Alfonso Ramírez's kids. The Ramírezes had moved into town a year ago and had rented the old Villa house when the octogenarian had passed on.

"Hey, Jimmy," I called out. But the young boy was lost in his own world, his tiny legs churning the wheels of the tricycle like miniature pistons as he made those motor sounds that young children make when they're alone with their intense and private fantasies. Jimmy reached the corner of Calle Mercado and turned down Calle Cuatro.

I knew the Ramírez family lived just three doors down, so I pulled my cruiser over and parked. As I got out of the patrol car I could see Jimmy riding his tricycle up the sidewalk to the front door of his home, one of the old craftsmen two-story wood-frame houses that had been built on Calle Cuatro in the thirties. Out of habit, I slid my baton into my belt harness, patted my gun and made my way to the house. The street was quiet, empty. The new mercury street lamps, that mayor Cervantes had pushed through the city council, cast an eerie purple aura over the entire block.

When I got to the house, I noticed that all the lights in the house were off. I noticed that many of the other houses on the block kept a front porch light on as a safety measure—but there was no porch light on here. And it was quiet, unusually quiet. Why was that? Suddenly it hit me, the constant chirp chirp of the cicadas that marked summers in Arroyo Grande had stopped. If there is one thing Arroyo Grande is famous for, it is oversized, rampantly in your face, cicadas, insects with no "off" button. Now, they were inexplicably silent.

Jimmy had disappeared through the front door, which remained ajar. I walked up to the porch and approached the door. It was too dark to see anything inside. I reached for my flashlight and turned it on, enveloping the front door in a pool of magna intense light. I peered inside but could see no one. Probably asleep upstairs, I thought.

I entered the house. In front of me were the worn wooden stairs that led to the bedrooms. To the right was an arched entrance leading to a modest dining room, and beyond that another door leading to the kitchen. To my left, another arched doorway leading to the living room, strewn with kids' toys, wrappers and empty pizza boxes, indicating a night of watching TV. Of course! Tonight had been the annual match-up between Texas A&M and UT Austin—a rivalry few people in Arroyo Grande missed.

"Hello," I said loudly. No answer.

Again, I called out. "Hello? Señor Ramírez? Anybody home?"

Silence.

Then I heard it. The make-believe engine sound I had heard Jimmy making on his tricycle, somewhere off in another room. I followed the sound. And then suddenly stopped. My foot had hit something. I shined the light down at my feet. It was Jimmy's tricycle. I thought I heard the noise coming again, seeming to come from behind the stairwell. I walked along the narrow corridor adjacent to the stairs that led to a back room. Then I saw it. There was a soft glow of light coming from a door underneath the stairs. I opened the door wider and peered in. I was looking down a long flight of stairs leading to a basement. At the bottom I could see that the light source was brighter. Something eerie about that light, not incandescent, not a light bulb, but not fluorescent either. Brighter but softer, a strange orange color. I was about to call out again, but that's when my cop instinct kicked in. There was something wrong here.

Why would little Jimmy be riding his tricycle along Calle Mercado at one o'clock in the morning? Why were all the lights out? Why was there no response. I knew that there were four children in the Ramírez household, in addition to Alfonso and his wife, Betty. Where was everybody?

Instinctively, I undid the hood on my revolver holster and started down the stairs. Suddenly it was very important for me to be quiet. I measured each step on the stairs carefully, allowing my weight to settle gradually on the wooden steps, spreading out my weight and muffling the creak on the old wooden planks. I descended slowly, carefully, keeping the light from my flashlight at my feet for obstacles but away from the bottom of the steps where it might give away my approach.

Half-way down the stairs, I began to hear it. A low, resonant moan, but a moan that seemed to come from more than one voice, as if two or three people were moaning together, in harmony. It was not a happy noise. It was rather a moan of pain, a moan of sorrow, of discord. Gradually, I got closer and closer to the bottom of the stairs. I turned off my flashlight and put it back on my belt—there was now more than enough light for me to see where I was stepping. The basement light was not only brighter but I could see that, indeed, it was a light unlike any I had ever seen before. The color of it, the orange and reddish hue, the magenta tinge. How it flickered and danced. Was it filters? Neon? I was dying to peek around the corner and see its source.

Finally, I was down at the last step. All I could see into the basement was the blank wall facing the stairs. To my right, the basement opened up into a large room, but I couldn't see what was in it. The moaning was much louder now, and, yes, it did seem to come from several voices. That's when I noticed two things, that my right hand was hurting from holding the gun so tightly (when had I pulled out my pistol?) and that I was drenched in sweat, the moisture descending from my cheeks and down to my neck and down my back. I stepped down from the last step and inched my head closer to the edge of the stairwell that hid the basement from view. The mystery of the room was just inches away from me. I prepared to peek around the corner. I held my breath and looked inside. What I saw made my skin crawl.

There were six of them. Alfonso Ramírez, his wife Betty and the four children, ranging in age from young Jimmy to six-year-old María, seven-year-old Stevie and nine-year-old Alfonso, Jr. They were all suspended about four feet off the ground—they were floating! Their arms were out-stretched, extended, with their fingers pointing out. They're mouths were wide open—that's where the moaning was coming from. A harmonic synthesis of six voices merging into one deep, uninterrupted moan. But what made my blood run cold was their eyes. They were wide open, but only the whites of their eyes were visible. Their eyeballs seemed to have disappeared inside their skulls.

Floating in the air with them were streams of blood and mucous, originating from their mouths, their eyes, their noses, their ears. The blood and bodily fluids floated and drifted, suspended in space, defying the laws of gravity. It reminded me of footage I had seen of liquids that astronauts had spilled while being weightless in space. The shimmering, iridescent light totally enveloped the six of them. It seemed to irradiate from them, fluctuating rhythmically with the breathing of the six members of the Ramírez family. I stared at this site for what seemed an eternity.

Suddenly, Jimmy's eyes descended from within his skull and he was staring directly at me. Suddenly, they had all regained their eyesight and were staring at me. Intensely, angrily, menacingly. I could feel their glare focused an inch behind my eyeballs. I was terrified.

Then young Jimmy floated in the air toward me. As he came closer and closer I instinctively took a step back. Then I noticed the hatred in his eyes, the stark, intense, angry hatred. How can a three-year-old hate so much? He came to rest directly in front of me, his face nose-to-nose with mine. He opened his mouth to speak, but instead of the trilling motor I had heard earlier, it was a man's voice—deep, raspy and angry.

"Don't!" he said emphatically. He dragged out the final syllable of the word into a hundred nuances of warning, threat and intimidation. "Doooooon't tell anyone!"

Jimmy settled to the ground, took my hand and led me up the stairs. He walked me to my patrol car, like an adult might lead a small child. Except, here I was the small child. Within minutes I was sitting in the driver's seat of my cruiser. Jimmy was on the sidewalk. He waved at me wordlessly, turned and started back into the house. I started up the cruiser and resumed my night of patrolling the streets of Arroyo Grande. I went through my routine as if nothing had happened. They call it "shock."

When I returned to the station, I went into the bathroom and washed off the sweat that had covered my face. Then I threw up, violently. When I was done, I went to one of the holding cells we keep for weekend drunks. I sat down in the empty cell and held my head in my hands. I was shaking all over, more frightened than I had ever been in my entire life.

A week later the Ramírez family moved out of town. I later asked Johnnie Mendoza of Arroyo Real Estate where they had gone.

He didn't know. "Damnest thing," he said to me, "Ramírez shows up one day with an envelope full of cash. They had taken out a three-year lease on the old house. They'd only lived there a little over a year. So here he is giving me the balance of the lease money, in cash! Said he had been promoted and was being relocated to another city. Last I saw of him!"

That was three years ago, and for all these years I've held it inside, but I haven't forgotten that night. There isn't a day that goes by that I don't relive the sight of the Ramírez family floating in the air, the mucous and the blood, the vacant stares, the moaning. And above all, the intense hatred in their eyes. A hatred directed at me but clearly originating from some terrible event that had shaped them or perhaps even had transformed them into that special, terrible thing that they were. Maybe they were that way before. I don't know. Perhaps they had always been like that. And who—what—were they, anyway? How could they have such abilities? To levitate their bodies? To make fluids float in the air? And the meaning of that horrible, visceral moaning? What was the meaning of that night and of what I had witnessed?

I've thought and thought about it and the only conclusion I am certain about is this. There exist on this earth things—call it a life force or entities or creatures or whatever you like. But these things are something that we know nothing about. Mysterious, sinister and evil things that live side by side with us, that walk our streets, that work next to us, that pretend they are just like us, except they're going about their hidden, secretive affairs. While we live our common, pedestrian lives, content in the knowledge that there is a God, that good does triumph over evil, that the laws of physics are inviolable, that the universe is as we know it, as science and history tell us it is.

And yet these creatures exist as living proof that all of our presumptuous beliefs and securities are sad, terrible, foolish delusions. For there are things in this world that are dark and hidden and evil. Unspeakable things that we know nothing about, that we do not understand. It is knowledge that, if we knew it, would drive us all mad with fear, and would send us screaming to the insane asylum. These things do exist. I know it because I saw it with my own two eyes. And that is why I can no longer sleep at night.

The last thing Bertha said to me before she left was, "Bobby, I love you. But you need the kind of help that I can't give you. You have a choice, either continue to let this delusion control you or go seek medical help. I beg you to seek help."

Well, this morning, after yet another nightmare, I made my decision. I called and made an appointment with the El Paso Psychiatry Center. I washed up and put on my best pants, shirt and tie and my brown wool jacket. I grabbed my keys and made sure the back door was locked. Then I headed for the front door and opened it.

My heartbeat stopped. There standing before me was Alfonso Ramírez. His eyes were vacant, like that night, just white where his eyeballs should have been. I stood frozen, fear suddenly racing through my body.

Then he spoke. "Where are you going, Bobby?"

BUILDERS OF THE NEW TEMPLO MAYOR

I become aware of sounds around me, slowly. Incremental sounds, distant sounds. And smells—pungent smells, pleasant smells, exotic smells, deep smells, metallic smells. Then the sounds come closer, louder. And the smells, stronger. But it's still all dark. Shouldn't there be light? Is it night? I start to make out words, someone says, "She's waking up." Then a blast of light in my right eye as someone peels back my eyelid. What the hell is going on?

"Jeannie, Jeannie, are you awake?"

"Huh," I say. Boy, do I feel groggy.

The light comes away from my eye and with it a rush of feelings: pain in my head, dry throat, aches on my back and arms, and lots and lots of different smells and aromas. A pinching feeling on my nose. I open my eyes and see that I'm lying on a bed in a hospital room with the walls painted a powder blue. In front of me, standing by the bed, is a nurse and a man dressed in a white doctor's smock. I'm confused.

"Jeannie, can you hear me?"

"Yes," I reply. "Where am I?"

"Great!" the man says, smiling.

"What's going on?" I ask.

"I'm Dr. Nardeem." He repeats it, "Dr. Nardeem."

"I have a headache. And I'm mighty, mighty thirsty. What are those smells? Can someone bring me some water."

"The headache is natural. It'll go away. Here's some ice, just suck on it for a while."

He gives me a cup of ice with a cotton mesh over it. I take it and try to suck through the cotton at the ice. The coolness is great!

"We've got to get you back gradually into drinking and eating," the doctor says. "You've been on intravenous fluids for two days."

I look around and see that I have an IV tube connected to my arm, a blood pressure cup clamped to my left index finger and a breathing catheter strapped across my nose. My hand touches bandages covering my head.

"What happened to me?"

"You've had an accident and have suffered a concussion. You've been in a coma for two days. How do you feel?"

Suddenly it all rushes back to me.

"Oh my God! Two days, I'm going to get fired! Don Carlos will fire me for sure this time. I gotta get back to the table!"

"The table?" Dr. Nardeem asks.

"The blackjack table. I'll lose my job. I can't afford to lose my job in this economy."

"Jeannie, I'm going to ask you a few questions. I need to see how badly the fall affected your thinking and your memory"

"I fell?"

"Yes, three stories. Quite a fall. Let's start with your name. What is your name?"

"Jeannie de la Cruz."

"Where do you live?"

"Why, here in Arroyo Grande, of course!"

Another doctor walks into the room just then. Dr. Nardeem turns to him. "John," he says, "you should listen to this."

"Jeannie, is Arroyo Grande in Arizona?"

"Of course not," I say, getting a little huffy. "Why would it be in Arizona? Arroyo Grande is in Texas where it's always been."

"What is your profession?"

"I'm a blackjack dealer at the casino."

"What's the name of the casino, Jeannie?"

What's going on here, why doesn't he know that? What kind of hospital am I in, anyway? Is this El Paso?

"The Arroyo Grande Casino and Sports complex," I answer him. "It's only the biggest gaming center in the state of Texas."

The two doctors exchange looks. They look concerned and *that* worries me.

"That was the wrong answer, wasn't it?"

"Jeannie, what's the last thing that you recall before waking up right now?"

"Let me think. I had gotten to work late, and Choo Choo Torres, he's the manager of the day shift at the casino, a real bastard son-of-a bitch, he yelled at me and said he'd have to report me to Don Carlos. Choo Choo said he hoped I would finally get fired, that there were other people waiting in line for a cozy job in this Depression. And then I went up the stairs to the second floor gaming tables. I could see Yoli Mendoza making the rounds. She's second-floor supervisor, monitors all of us dealers and she's a real bitch. We used to be friends once, but not now I just stay out of her way. A real bitch! I started getting ready to open up my table. And that's when I saw Don Carlos coming toward me. He looked pretty pissed off. But then he's always pissed off at one thing or another. Ever since he got demoted. I knew then that Choo Choo must have squealed on me."

"Jeannie do you recall falling?"

"That's it!" I said, suddenly remembering. "I got up and started to walk up the winding staircase to the third floor. I figured maybe I could get away from Don Carlos before he started yelling at me, give him time to cool down. He always likes to make an example of people, in front of the other workers. The day before, he made Max Martínez, the janitor, pick up some trash he had accidentally spilled and was shouting and swearing at him the whole time. Poor Max, he just sucked it up, but I could tell he was swearing inside. I guess I must've lost my footing going up the stairs. Is that what happened? Did I fall down the casino staircase?"

"Jeannie, have you ever heard of Pirámide Enterprises?"

"No, what is that?"

"Have you ever been in Tucson, Arizona?"

At that I immediately start to tear up. "Yes," I blurt out, trying to hold back the tears. The doctor picks up on that. "Why are you crying, Jeannie? Did something bad happen in Tucson?"

"Yes," I say. All of sudden I'm reliving Mexico City and that horrible night.

"The funeral," I say in between sobs. "That's where I buried my . . . my life partner, Gale Watson." Then I just let it go. I start to bawl. The nurse comes over and cradles me in her arms.

Dr. Nardeem nods to the doctor named John and whispers something I can't make out.

"I'll get her," the other doctor says.

The nurse hands me some Kleenex and when I lift my head to wipe my nose, my heart explodes. There, walking through the door into the room is my Gale! Alive! She runs to my side and embraces me. She looks into my eyes with that look of love I haven't seen in years.

"Oh, my dear *macushla*," she says, "are you okay?"

"Gale, you're here," I can hear myself say. It's all like a dream. "You're alive!"

"Of course, I'm here. And why wouldn't I be alive? *Macushla*, I've been at your side for the past two days since your fall."

Macushla, she calls me. Gaelic for "my love." It *is* Gale! It is definitely Gale. She always called me *macushla* and I always called her "*amorcito*."

I still can't believe my eyes. Gale alive! And Gale smells so wonderful! I start to cry all over again. Suddenly I get very sleepy. So very sleepy. I can feel my eyelids dropping.

"Let her sleep," I hear someone say.

* * *

"Jeannie, are you awake?"

I open my eyes and see Gale sitting in a chair next to my hospital bed. The sun is shining through an open window, but the angle and color of the light has shifted. It must be afternoon. The two doctors and the nurse I saw before are standing behind Gale. It all comes back to me now in a rush, the fall from the Casino staircase, waking up in the hospital with doctors questioning me and then seeing Gale. Gale alive!

"Gale, it's true you are alive! I thought I was dreaming."

"Of course, I'm alive. And, thank God, so are you. In spite of your fall."

"I fell?" I ask, still trying to make sense of what has happened to me.

"From the pyramid," Gale says. "You were supervising construction on the south side of the foundation. You got too close to the edge and fell off. Rudy Vargas and Bobby Hernández brought you here to the university hospital."

"I don't remember any of that!" I confess. I'm quiet for a moment and touch Gale's face. "Oh Gale, how can you be . . . alive?"

"Huh," she says. "Sweetie, why wouldn't I be alive?"

I shake my head, then look to the doctors. "Am I going crazy?"

Doctor Nardeem steps closer to me.

"Jeannie, we have to tell you some things that are going to come as a shock to you," he says. He puts his hand on my arm trying to reassure me.

"Now listen carefully. Two days ago, you fell off a three-story ledge at a construction site a few miles outside of Tucson, Arizona. That's where we're at now, in the intensive care unit of the University of Arizona Hospital. We've run MRIs and other tests and have determined that your brain was severely damaged, specifically the medial temporal lobe, and more specifically the hippocampus—that's the part of the brain that is responsible for emotions, long term memory and olfaction . . . what you smell."

"My brain was damaged?" I ask, taking it all in.

"Here's what we know," he continues. "Your procedural memory, your ability to talk and move your hands and process conversation and sounds, was unaffected. That's good news. But your memory of your own life, we call it episodic memory and your knowledge of facts about the world at large, we call that semantic memory, seems to have been affected in a way we haven't really encountered before."

What is he getting at?

"You're not the first person to have brain damage in the hippocampus part of the brain. Typically, the result is amnesia of some sort. People either can't remember events that happened before the trauma took place, or they have trouble making and remembering new memories, things that happened since the accident."

"So which one do I have?"

"Your case is very special. You have created a *false* memory of events that never happened at all! But because you were damaged in the part of the brain that controls emotions and long term memory, your false memories will feel like real memories."

"Doctor," I say, "that's exactly how I feel. I *know* I was a blackjack dealer at the casino. And this hospital seems all wrong. But my Gale is alive."

"Do you now recall her being alive in your false memory?"

"She was dead in what you call my false memory. I *know* that. I buried her! She died in my arms in Mexico City!"

At this point Gale gets a horrified look on her face.

"Jeannie," the doctor says, "I would just ask you not to make any judgment on things just yet. Remember your brain has been severely traumatized, you're still recovering. Just take it easy for a while."

"But what about Arroyo Grande and the casino and my job? How can I have made that up? It's all so vivid. I know I lived that life! How can I not be crazy?"

"You're not crazy, Jeannie," he replies. "Just badly hurt. Our prognosis is that eventually you'll get your real memories back. But we're not sure how long that will take. We're going to keep you here a few days and run more tests. We hope to have more answers for you soon. In the meantime, Gale is here for you."

"Yes, I'm here for you," Gale says, giving me another hug. "Always."

My god, Gale is alive!

* * *

The next morning, after a night of long and deep sleep, I'm ready to compare notes with Gale. I want to find out how much of what I remember is true and how much my mind has evidently made up.

"Gale," I tell her. "Indulge me. I'll tell you all that I remember and you tell me what part of that is real, and what part of it my mind is making up because of the accident. Okay?"

"Of course, *macushla*."

"First, I was born in Arroyo Grande and went to Jefferson High School there before getting a scholarship to MIT, where I majored in engineering with a minor in architecture. I finished my four years and got a Fulbright to study the architectural engineering of Meso-American civilizations for modern-day applications."

"That's right. That's where we met. I was also on that dig."

"Yes, in Mexico City . . . "

" . . . at the ruins of the Templo Mayor," Gale finishes the thought for me. "We were studying with Dr. Armendáriz there."

"Please, Gale, let me do it. Yes, *we* were studying under Prof. Armendáriz, expert on the early civilization of Tenochotitlán and the construction of the Aztec Templo Mayor before it was destroyed by the Spanish. You were a graduate student at the University of Arizona then, and Prof. Armendáriz had hit on you several times and you were getting ready to leave the dig."

"You got that right, Jeannie. And that's when I met you."

"Gale, let me tell it, please. I gotta make sure it's my memories. You're from Arizona . . . Tucson?"

"Right, Tucson."

"We fell in love and had a wonderful summer exploring Mexican ruins and partying mighty, mighty hardy in the Zona Rosa. We had several close Mexican friends, including María Platero and her partner Neti Vásquez. And then, just before we were to head back to the States, you got a phone call from a Mr. Zapata. He offered you a job in Tucson, and we were making plans to travel together . . . when the accident happened."

"What accident?"

Here's where it gets a little tricky. I start to tear up again. I get so damn emotional!

"Gale, you and I were walking across Paseo de la Reforma. We were going to a concert at Bellas Artes. We were late and you were running just a few feet ahead of me. You turned back to tell me to hurry up, when you were hit by a speeding taxi. The bastard never even slowed down. When I got to your side, I could see you were all broken up. You had fractures in your leg and arms, everywhere. You were unconscious, your head was mangled and smashed. I held you in my arms, and before they could even call for an ambulance, you died. Right there in my arms."

"Whoa! Really? I died?! I can't believe it! No wonder you were surprised to see me yesterday."

"That's why I kept crying when I saw you next to me. Gale, I love you. But I remember burying you in the cemetery in Tucson. You're parents, Sarah and Henry, were there, and many of your high school and university friends. Everyone loved you so much."

"What happened after that?" Gale was all ears now.

"I went into a deep depression. Everything I had ever wanted to do in engineering and in life was tied to you. I had no more heart for engineering, not with you gone. So I went back home to Arroyo Grande. Two months later, the market tanked when the housing bubble burst. It ushered in the second greatest depression in US history. Massive. People jumping out of buildings, riots, marshal law. Within a year and half, the entire economic landscape in the country had changed. Unemployment skyrocketed, people lost their homes, their jobs and any chance at a future. Most of the gang I grew up with, Choo Choo Torres, Yoli Mendoza, Reymundo Salazar, Bobby Hernández, all of them came home to help out with their families."

"Honey, you have some imagination. And you're 'remembering' all of this?"

"Like it was yesterday," I tell her. And I mean it.

"The only one that benefitted from the Second Great Depression, everyone called it the SGD," I continue, "was those bastards at Rebber and Barrón who took advantage of the situation and bought up bank loans and soon started foreclosing on all the homes in the barrio. They had a master plan for Arroyo Grande. It turns out the building of that enormous skyscraper in Arroyo Grande and later the convention center was just the beginning. They envisioned turning Arroyo Grande into a giant casino and sports complex. They wanted to make Arroyo Grande bigger than Las Vegas!"

Gale is really mesmerized now. "And they succeeded?"

"Of course. Working with their cronies in the state legislature, they passed a special law that gave Arroyo Grande priority gambling privileges in Texas. But they waited until the first part of the casino complex was nearly completed before they rammed it through, guaranteeing that the Arroyo Grande casino would be way ahead of any other gambling ventures in Texas."

It was all sinking in to Gale by now. "And you went to work for the casino as a blackjack dealer?"

"Hey, with unemployment running at forty percent in Texas, everyone in Arroyo Grande went to work for the casino. My doctorate didn't mean a thing in the new economy. The lucky ones like Choo Choo Torres, Yoli Mendoza and Junior Valdez got jobs as managers—they turned out to be real assholes. The rest of us got jobs as dealers, or in the kitchens or like Max Martínez and the Maldonado Brothers—they lost their auto shop with the Depression—as janitors and groundskeepers.

"Wow," Gale exclaims, cradling my face in her hands. "My honey, you have a very vivid imagination." She kisses me tenderly and we hug. I hold on like my whole life depends on this one hug. Finally, I feel much better.

"But none of that is true," I ask. "Right?"

"Right, thank God!"

"Honey, see if you remember any of these events. We did come back to Tucson after Mexico City. We decided to move in together. The guy that called me with the job offer, his name is Manuel Zapata. We knew him as the Recruiter. He got me and you a job for a new enterprise they were building outside of Tucson—a giant pyramid in the middle of the desert. It's a crazy concept, but he's managed to get people from all over the world to work on it. My job was working in design, engineering and implementation. You sit me before a drafting table and I am a happy camper. But you're more outgoing and you have excellent people skills. It didn't take long for Zapata to see this, and you were soon put in charge of supervising construction of the pyramid foundation. I remember the night he made you the offer. You came home so excited. We celebrated by going out to our favorite restaurant, El Minuto, and getting thoroughly soused. You don't remember any of that?"

"I wish I did," I said. "Sounds like I missed out on a real great time! How long have we lived together?"

"We got married a year after we came to Tucson. That was three years ago."

"I've lost four years?"

"Honey, you did live it! You just can' remember it right now. But the doctor said it would probably all come back to you soon."

"*Amorcito*," I say to Gale, "you don't know how much I want to remember those years you say I've lived with you. And boy do I want to forget the terrible memories of what life was like without you. I hated going to work every day, sitting at that table dealing cards to a parade of assholes and jerks. All the men making private side bets to see who could bed me first. Ugh! When will these memories leave me?"

"Let's ask the doctor when you see him tomorrow."

* * *

"Not sure what to tell you, Jeannie," Dr. Nardeem says, reviewing a set of X-rays of my brain at a light box on the hospital room wall. "It may take a month or a year, and you may never fully lose a sense of these false memories."

Not what I want to hear, believe me!

"As I said before," he continues, "the bulk of the literature on hippocampus injuries documents amnesia of one kind or another. Your case is something we've not seen before. Evidently, the neural processes we associate with creativity tapped into your episodic and semantic memories and reconfigured them as false memories. But these false memories evidently feel just as real as the recent memories you've had since you woke up from the accident. I expect that as your recent memories get transferred to long-term memory storage, you'll be forgetting the false memories."

He comes over and reads the chart that the nurse has handed him.

"Studies have shown that the more we revisit a particular memory, the more it gets ingrained into long-term memory storage. Other long-term memories, that don't get resurrected as often, soon drift away. We forget them. What's left are the very vivid memories that we have recalled time and time again. That's why older people tell the same story about their youth over and over again, and these are usually positive stories. The bad things that happen to us we try to forget—can't blame us. In your case, from what you've told me, your false memories are not very pleasant. So you probably won't be recalling them too often from memory storage, and we can only hope they'll gradually fade away."

"Is there anything she can do to help this process?" Gale asks.

"Yes, there is. The more you recall recent, pleasant memories and strive *not* to recall your unpleasant false memories, the better off you'll be."

"But what if these false memories really took place?" I ask. I just can't get them out of my mind. They seem so real. "Aren't I cheating? I mean, aren't I denying the validity of these events?"

"Jeannie, the point is you must not allow the bad memories of a terrible past to cripple you and your future. It's as simple as that."

* * *

So I go back to work at the pyramid three months after the accident, and they have a big welcome back party for me. When I see Manuel Zapata, I have an instant moment of deja vu. Is my memory starting to come back? I learn that we called ourselves Builders of the New Templo Mayor, that Zapata is the director of Pirámide Enterprises and that the projected date for completing the pyramid is 2045. Wow, quite a mighty, mighty long way off.

I'm so happy to see my old friends Rudy Vargas, Bobby Hernández and Robert and Johnnie Rodríguez. Gale had told them about my false memory and suggested they remind me about how they had got to work for Pirámide Enterprises. It turns out I had recruited *all of them* from Arroyo Grande and—this is really hard for me to swallow—that I'm their boss! Rudy works in communications, the Rodríguez brothers head up construction and I hired Bobby as head of security. He takes me aside and says confidentially, "Jeannie, thanks again for believing in me after my break-down." His breakdown? I don't have a clue.

Seeing my old friends prompts me to place a call to Yoli Mendoza, whom Gale informs me is living in the Chelsea art district of New York City. The conversation starts awkwardly. She's all friendly and not all the bitch I recall from my false memory. Turns out we've maintained our friendship over all of these years, and she's actually visited me and Gale. By the end of the conversation, we're joking and laughing the way we did when we were in high school. She tells me that she's still in touch with Choo Choo Torres, but that they're just friends now. But Choo Choo is about to start his first major motion picture for Paramount based on his student short about lowrider zombies that he shot in Arroyo Grande. Yoli reminds me of the great time we had at her one-woman show at the Sasonz Gallery. She chuckles that I must keep my promise not to tell anyone about Mrs. Romero's portrait and *you know what*.

I can't remember what the hell she's talking about.

* * *

Well, it's been six months since the accident. And I can tell you I am having the time of my life! I love my work at the pyramid—damn it, we *will* have it completed by the year 2045! And my life with Gale is all that I had hoped it would be. Even better than our days in Mexico City! Yes, every now and then I get a dèjá vu moment, or I'll recall a terrible false memory. But when that happens, I do what Dr. Nardeem suggested I do.

I try to forget it.

Instead, I revisit a pleasant memory of my life with Gale. If it's a choice between one, remembering I was an unhappy blackjack dealer where Yoli and Choo Choo were complete assholes or, two, being happy in the present with a very much alive and loving Gale, hey, I'll take number two any day.

I mean, wouldn't you?

AN EPHEMERAL ALDERMAN

"The first time I remembered it happening to me, I was going to a city council meeting at City Hall. I remember walking into the men's room and going to the urinal. The room was empty. Of that I am certain."

The man stopped speaking for a moment and wiped sweat from his forehead with a rumpled handkerchief. He took a tentative sip of water from the glass I'd given him.

"When I had finished," he continued, "and turned around, I saw this old man, a janitor. He was mopping the floor. The bathroom floor was filled with soapy water and there was one of those yellow folding signs blocking the bathroom entrance. But just a minute ago neither the janitor nor the mop nor the sign had been there. I'd been at the urinal with my back turned for less than a minute, so how'd the janitor accomplish all that work in such a short time?"

He took another sip of water and I could see his hand was shaking. He continued his story.

"I got a bigger surprise when I walked out of the bathroom and found the hallway, that only a few minutes ago had been full of people, was now completely empty. I looked out the windows that lit the hallway and saw that it was dark outside. It was night. Yet when I'd walked into the restroom, just minutes before, the afternoon sun had been streaming through those windows. Somehow I had lost several hours of the day."

I hadn't seen Charlie Villalobos this bad since I had started treating him for depressive anxiety syndrome almost two years ago. He was one of my first patients when I opened up my practice on Calle Cinco. I thought that we had made great progress and that he had gotten control of the terrible guilt he felt following the accident. I had even curtailed our weekly sessions to meeting once a month. But now Charlie, and his anxiety, were back with a vengeance.

"Go on, Charlie," I prodded gently, "you said this has happened several times?"

He moistened his lips and continued.

"About a week later, it was a Friday morning. I'd just finished giving a speech to the Arroyo Grande Chamber of Commerce and I was on my way to my car—late for my next appointment. I remember opening the car door and settling into the seat. The next thing I know, I hear the blaring of car horns. I'm sitting in the car, but somehow the car is now at the intersection of Calle Cinco and Sycamore, and the light is green and people behind me are leaning on their horns for me to drive on through the intersection. I did, of course, and then quickly pulled the car over to the side and parked. I was terrified. I remembered getting into the car but not driving to the intersection. Somehow I'd gotten through ten blocks of traffic without remembering. Once again I had lost time."

The car association made sense, I thought to myself, it's all about the accident. All those who were gathered outside the Maldonado Brothers garage on that fateful summer day, all who had witnessed the tragedy, agreed that it was simply an unavoidable accident. Choo Choo Torres, home for the summer following his last year at USC, had been so preoccupied with filming for his zombie movie that he had unwittingly backed into the street right in front of Charlie's car. Observers all agreed that there was no way Charlie could have braked in time to avoid hitting Choo Choo. The tragedy had hit Charlie really hard. One of the sponsors of our baseball team, the Arroyo Grande Sluggers, Charlie had known Choo Choo since he was eleven years old. I'm sure this contributed greatly to his sense of guilt for Choo Choo's death.

"And you say it's getting worse?" I asked.

"When it first started, I would lose a few hours of time. A few hours where I couldn't remember what had happened. All of a sudden I would find myself in a different location and I couldn't remember what had brought me there or what had transpired before; however, the last time it happened, I lost a whole day! I remember going into council chambers early one morning. I was reviewing notes for the speech I was going to give. The next thing I remember was waking up in my bed the *next day*."

"You can't remember what happened to you for a whole day?"

"When I got to my office the next day, my assistant came up to me and congratulated me on the great speech I'd given at the council meeting the day before. She told me that it was one of the best speeches I had ever delivered . . . but I couldn't remember saying a word! That afternoon I went to the city clerk's office and asked to see a replay of my speech—they videotape each council meeting. Sure enough, there I was, big as life, giving this passionate speech about stopping runaway development in Arroyo Grande and how we should stop the expansion plans of the Rebber and Barrón Casino Project. I looked at that videotape but it was like watching a stranger."

"Charlie, you looked really startled when I opened the door a few minutes ago."

"You noticed! Listen to this: the last thing I remember before you opened the door was going to bed last night feeling very worried, worried that it would happen again. I turned off the bedroom light, kissed Yolanda goodnight, and the next thing I remember, I was standing outside the lobby here, staring at your sign, 'Antonio Valdez, Jr. Psychotherapy.' That's when you opened the door and said, 'You can come in now.'

"Charlie, you called me yesterday to set up the appointment. You don't remember calling me?"

"No, not a thing. Junior—you don't mind me calling you Junior?"

"You know you can always call me Junior."

"So, Junior, am I going crazy?"

I walked over to him and put my arms around his shoulders. "Charlie," I said, "the human mind is a fantastic, complicated mechanism. In spite of modern science, we still don't completely understand its complex workings. But we do know that when stressed by deep feelings, profound emotions, there is no telling what the mind can do."

"You think this is all about . . . "

"Of course. In spite of the two years we've spent in therapy going over this, you still feel enormously guilty for Choo Choo's death. Your mind accepts the facts: Choo Choo Torres walks backwards into the street, his attention so riveted on his filming that he doesn't realize he is walking into traffic. You come driving by—and remember, you weren't speeding—yet you have no time to brake. Now, your mind accepts the logic of these facts, and that it was *not* your fault. But your emotional side can't shake the guilt. Good grief, it's been five years since his death and you still have an overpowering sense of culpability—in your subconscious mind it *wasn't* an accident, *you* caused his death. Facts collide with emotion—you're in a stalemate, a deadlock. So your mind finds a creative way to deal with this, to deflect the guilt, to get you off the hook."

"But what does this have to do with these blackouts?"

"Apply what's happening to you now to the Choo Choo accident. If there are moments when you black out, when you don't remember what happened, then it follows that there are moments in your life when you are not responsible for your actions. Your actions become the actions of a 'stranger,' isn't that how you phrased it?"

"My God!" Charlie said as the realization sunk in. "So these blackouts are me attempting to deny that I was responsible for Choo Choo's death."

"I think so, or something pretty close to it. From what you've told me about your work schedule, it also sounds like you're overworked. I wouldn't rule out stress as a factor here. In our modern age, a lot of us get the sense that life is going by too fast. You know, you start out in the morning to get a lot of things done and before you know it its evening, you haven't done half the things you set out to do. There's just too much happening in our modern world—information overload. These blackouts could also be your way of coping with that."

Charlie nodded and for the first time, I sensed relief in him.

"Look," I continued, "you need to take a few days off from city council and unwind a bit. Spend some time with Yolanda. Get a babysitter, go to a movie—there's that new comedy with Julia Miranda just opened up at the Fox. Our hometown girl made good, huh? In other words, Charlie, relax."

"Thanks, Junior, say—all about me—how's your family?"

"Toño Junior just entered kindergarten, and Sarita's all about her Brownie troop, and Lupe . . . well, you know, Lupe is Lupe! Thanks for asking. Look, Charlie, I want you to come back in a week. I'm going to give you a prescription, a mild sedative to quiet your nerves. Take one in the morning and one in the evening."

As I walked him to the door, he stopped for a moment and looked up at the lobby wall where I had hung the framed Intergalactic Lasergun and Extraterrestrial Voice-decoder that I had hauled out of Mrs. Romero's sinkhole so many years ago.

"Hey, I remember that thing!" Charlie said. "You used to walk around with it all the time when we were kids."

"Yeah, I got it out of . . . "

"Mrs. Romero's sinkhole!" he finished for me, then he stopped and pulled out a magnifying glass from his coat pocket.

"Look at this. It's a magnifying glass with a light that allows you to illuminate whatever it is you're looking at." He pushed a button on the magnifying glass handle and a tiny light came on. "That's what *I* got from Mrs. Romero's sinkhole. I'd forgotten I even had it until about six months ago when my eyesight started going bad. I dug it up and now I use it all the time—to read fine print on city documents, restaurant menus, you name it. It works great!"

"Restaurant menus?"

"Waitresses can't help but laugh when I use it, but, heck, it works!"

"I guess we all got something out of that old hole in the ground."

"Why'd you frame it?" he asked, nodding to the wall.

"A keepsake," I lied. Charlie didn't need to know that I keep it there to remind me of why I had chosen psychiatry as a profession.

"Charlie," I said, as I ushered him out the door, "remember to take the pills and just focus on relaxing. It's okay to relax."

* * *

Two days later I received another call from Charlie. He sounded really panicked. He asked me to see him as soon as possible. I agreed. Then he asked me what day of the week it was, and I told him it was Tuesday. He began sobbing on the other end of the phone. That really alarmed me. I told him I'd stay late and see him that evening.

It was almost eight o'clock in the evening before Charlie showed up. At first, I thought he was drunk. He looked disheveled and was slurring his words.

"Junior," he said, clasping my hand and not letting go. "You're still here!"

"I'm here for you, Charlie," I replied as I directed him to the couch. "Sit down."

"You don't understand!" he said emphatically, suddenly wresting his arm from my hands.

I'm not crazy! Now I know what's happening. And that's the worse part of it . . . I'm not crazy!"

"Charlie, sit down. What have you figured out?"

"I know what's happening to me! I know why I'm blacking out and losing days."

"Tell me about it, Charlie."

I tried not to project my feelings but wondered if I would have to call El Paso Psychiatric Care before the night was out. I had never seen Charlie in this condition before. I doubted that he would get violent, but it *had* happened to me once before, with another patient. And it had taken the emergency boys an hour and a half to get to me, although El Paso was only fifty minutes away. I was really worried about him.

Charlie settled onto the couch and shook his head as if confirming something to himself. "Junior, this is what I think is happening." Then he stopped. He was having difficulty trying to organize his thoughts.

Finally he spoke. "I think that I'm someone's dream."

I could see that he had chosen each word carefully.

He repeated himself. "I think that I'm someone's dream." He articulated each word with precision, clarity and finality, as if he was dictating an obituary.

"You're having someone's dream?"

"No, I *am* someone's dream!"

He went on. "The reason that I lose time is because I'm a dream in progress. You know, like when you have a dream and wake up for a moment and then go back to sleep and resume the dream you were having. Well, that's what I think is happening here. Someone is dreaming me and my life. And every now and then, this person or thing or whatever it is turns in his sleep. And when he wakes up for that brief moment, I no longer exist. For that moment when he's no longer dreaming, I cease to be. So I lose time. Then he goes back to the dream, and I resume my life. You see what I mean? It all makes sense!"

Now he really had me worried. I had read of cases of delusional solipsism, but had never encountered a case in person. Now, here it was. And it appeared to be an outgrowth of the depressive anxiety that had brought him to me in the first place. Fifty-six-year-old Charlie Villalobos, a respected member of Arroyo Grande, a city alderman, a sponsor of baseball teams, education drives and relief for the homeless. A happily married man with three young children. And here he was, coming apart at the seams believing that he was nothing more than the figment of someone's imagination, a dream that some person or cosmic entity was dreaming.

"And now you must know why I am terrified," he said, suddenly grabbing my arm and staring deep into my eyes.

"Charlie, please calm down."

"No!" he insisted, digging his nails into my forearm. "You know what this means, don't you? You know why I'm so . . . scared!" He clutched my arm harder as he broke down in tears.

"Junior, what's going to happen to me when this person wakes up? When this person wakes up from his dream, I'll cease to be! That'll be the end of me!

* * *

I spent the next hour trying to reason with Charlie and bring him back to *terra firma*.

"Charlie, let's go back to why you came to me in first place. Do you remember?"

"Choo Choo."

"Right. Now, look at the logic of this delusion you're having. It's what we talked about before. If you're the product of someone's dream, then you're not responsible for your actions. The person dreaming you is creating you and your actions. So it wasn't you that accidentally killed Choo Choo, it was this dreamer that caused you to do this. You see, *blame displacement*. Your mind is trying to get you off the hook. Your subconscious cares an awful lot for you and is trying all it can to get you off your self-imposed guilt trip. And, this is *really* ingenious. If your dreamer wakes up and you cease to be, then you didn't kill Choo Choo because none of your life really happened. You never existed, so you couldn't have killed Choo Choo Torres. If you cease to exist, then Choo Choo Torres is alive and well. Choo Choo never died."

"I'd rather kill myself than know that I killed him."

"Exactly my point."

He was silent. I could see the idea was sinking in. He slowly started to nod his head in agreement.

"Charlie," I continued, driving home my point, "do you see how silly this all seems? If your whole existence is nothing more than someone's dream, then doesn't it follow that not only are you a part of that dream but so am I, and all of the people of Arroyo Grande, and the grand state of Texas, and the United States of America. Yes, and the world and the universe. If you cease to be when this dreamer wakes up, doesn't that mean that the whole universe as we know it will cease to be?"

"No," he said with a sincerity that unsettled me. "Just me."

"Why just you?" I was really intrigued at the depth and complexity of his delusion.

"Because I'm the only one that is having these blackouts, that's why! The rest of the world, you and everyone else in Arroyo Grande will go on with your normal lives, except you'll do it without me. It'll be as if I never existed."

Now that stopped me. I had to admit to myself that Charlie's subconscious mind was not only working overtime but was putting on a brilliant academy award-winning performance of convoluted creativity and self-reinforcing rationale. How could you argue with the logic of his argument?

"Charlie," I said, reasserting my authority as the mental practitioner, "you're overworked and stressed out. You need to rest. What about that vacation with Yolanda?"

"Yeah, we talked about it . . . she thought I was crazy at first. A vacation in the middle of the school year, without the kids?"

"Well, you're not crazy. Get a relative to watch over the kids, go have that vacation with Yolanda. That's an order from your shrink. Charlie, you have a choice!"

* * *

I didn't hear from Charlie for several days and that was just fine—I was having my own set of troubles. Since the death of my father a year ago, the development firm of Rebber and Barrón had made offers for me to sell the building in which dad had operated Valdez Grocery Store for more than three decades. For me, the old homestead had deep meaning. It was here that I had grown up. I had both fond memories of living upstairs from the grocery store, and also deeply bitter memories. It was here that I won my first mental health victory, battling with my dad's alcoholism and eventually getting him to give up the drink.

It really wasn't until my freshman year at ASU, sitting in Dr. Gary Keller's psychology class, when I first heard about psychological denial, projection and fantasy fugues, that I came to understand just how deeply troubled I had been as a child. In trying to deny my dad's verbal and physical abuse on our family—always instigated by the bottle—I had pretended to be a space alien occupying the body of a Mexican-American kid named Junior Valdez. This fantasy world I created spared me from having to acknowledge my father's cruelty. When I finally got my father to stop drinking, I was able to let go of my fantasies.

But it was in that hot psychology lecture hall in Tempe, Arizona, that I resolved that psychology would be my calling. Perhaps I would be able to do something so that some other child would never have to go through what I had gone through. Or perhaps I would just simply help people deal with their inner demons. Either way I knew that psychotherapy was my calling. That's why I had hung up my old Intergalactic Lasergun and Extraterrestrial Voice-decoder on the wall of my office. As a reminder.

And as for Rebber and Barrón, no way was I going to sell the old homestead. They could go to hell!

* * *

Two weeks passed and I didn't hear from Charlie, so I figured that he must have taken my advice and that he and

Yolanda had gone on a nice vacation. Then I got an urgent message from him on my phone.

"Junior," the recording said, "it's started again. And this time I know I'm right. He's waking up, Junior, he's waking up and I'm going to die soon. Junior, help me! Help me!"

Of course I immediately called him back. But the home number I had was disconnected. Now that worried me a lot. When someone is suicidal, one of the first things they do is try to break off any connection with the world as they know it. I tried to track him down through his office at City Hall. Once I explained who I was, I was certain they'd give me his home phone number. And that's when I got my first big shock. The secretary for the Arroyo Grande City Council said she had never heard of Charlie Villalobos.

"What do you mean you haven't heard of Charlie Villalobos? He's a city alderman, for chrissake! Don't you have a listing of city aldermen?"

"We do, sir," the secretary replied indignantly, "and I have that list right in front of me and there's no one by that name listed."

"Look," I said, deciding to take a different tact, "can you connect me with Nancy Cervantes."

"Mayor Cervantes, yes, of course. Just a minute please."

Well, it took more than a minute but eventually I got Nancy Cervantes on the line.

"Nancy, it's me, Antonio Valdez."

"Junior! What a pleasant surprise. So good to hear from you. And how's the practice going, and how's Lupe and the kids?"

"Practice is fine, Lupe is fine, thank you. And the kids are great. Listen, Nancy, this is a bit of an emergency. Do you have a home number for Charlie Villalobos?"

"Who?"

"Charlie, Charlie Villalobos, as in alderman of the Fourth Ward."

"Junior, are you pulling my leg? Ed Carrillo is the alderman for the Fourth Ward. I'm afraid I don't know who you're talking about. Charlie Villalobos doesn't ring a bell."

About that time I felt the hairs on the back of my neck stand on edge.

"Nancy," I said, "humor me. You're telling me you never heard of anyone named Charlie Villalobos?"

"Junior, the first time I heard that name was two minutes ago when you called."

My mind was a jumble. What the hell was going on here?

"Nancy, remember back when Mrs. Ybarra claimed to have seen the Virgin of Guadalupe in her back yard?"

"Of course, wasn't that a wacky time!"

"Nancy who was the alderman that called for an 8 PM curfew for anyone under fifteen years of age?"

"Ed Carrillo, he was running for mayor against Al Snyder."

Jesus! Was *I* going crazy now? I knew in my heart of hearts that it was Charlie Villalobos who had run against Snyder! I thanked Nancy for her time and hung up. There was no need to alarm her with what I was sure would appear to be some pretty bizarre questions. I needed to think this through. I knew that someone doesn't just disappear off the face of the earth. There had to be a record of the existence of one Carlos Alejandro Villalobos.

For the next three hours, I sat at my computer and systematically checked all possible leads. I started with the Arroyo Grande City Hall website. As the city clerk had told me, I found no listing of Charlie in the city council or, for that matter, in any city department. Next, I googled Charlie's name in all its variations—Carlos, Chuck, Carl, Charlie. Eight listings came up, four for Carlos Alejandro Villalobos in Mexico, one in Costa Rica, one in Venezuela and three in Spain. None of them the Charlie I knew.

Then I got a brainstorm. Charlie'd have to be listed in the newspaper account of Choo Choo Torres' death. I pulled up the *Arroyo Grande Times* website and searched for past stories with Charlie's name. There was nothing. Then I went for broke and searched the newspaper archives for the day after Choo Choo's death. A replica of the Arroyo Grande masthead appeared and along with it a listing of all the articles in that day's paper. But something was missing. I had clipped that article and had filed it away in my diary—the front page of the paper had a big photo of Choo-Choo Torres with the headline, "Native Son Killed in Tragic Accident." But there was no photo and no headline. I systematically scanned each page of the paper and read each article. I broke out in a sweat when I realized that there was not one mention of the death of Choo Choo Torres!

And that's when my phone rang.

I picked it up, my mind still trying to fathom what possibly could have happened to Charlie Villalobos. "Hello," I said, "Dr. Antonio Valdez."

The voice on the other end of the phone was as familiar as my face in the mirror, a voice I hadn't heard for five years. And perhaps that's why I couldn't suppress the sob that erupted from deep within me.

"Choo-Choo?" I asked incredulously.

"Yeah, Junior. This is Choo Choo Torres! I'm calling to see if you'll be able to make it to the screening of my film *Attack of the Lowrider Zombies*. You know, the USC senior thesis that I was able to get a studio deal with Paramount to reshoot as a feature. It's finished now, and we're doing a special pre-screening before its national release, down at the Fox theater tomorrow night. A way of thanking everyone in Arroyo Grande who helped me out. Do you think you can make it?"

I stared at the phone in silence, trying to grapple with something that was simply unbelievable: Choo Choo Torres, my childhood friend, was alive! A thousand thoughts jumbled into my mind and fought for a hearing as I tried to make sense of it all. Then I experienced memory flashes of acting in Choo Choo's film. I was a zombie ghoul that went berserk in the supermarket. But where did that memory come from?

After a long silence, Choo Choo spoke up. "Junior, you still there?"

"Yes, Choo Choo, I'm here. And I'll be there for the screening. Damn well count on it!"

And that is when I lost it. I hung up the phone and just broke down. I took the same advice I often gave to patients on the verge: I cried and sobbed and just let it come out. There was clearly an irreconcilable confusion deep within me, this deep hurt, this chaos, this madness, had to get out. So I cried it out.

Later, I tried to reason it out, but what role did reason have in this?

Had Charlie Villalobos really existed? And if so, was I to believe that there was some greater reality in which we were all pawns, all the stuff of dreams? Was I to believe that Charlie Villalobos could exist one day and then be gone the next? Or was I to believe that I had made it all up. That there had never been a Charlie Villalobos and that I had made him *and* his psychosis up. That, after years of schooling, I had a mental break down and was once again creating a delusional world like the one I had created when I was a child and thought of myself as an alien in the body of Antonio Valdez, Jr. And to what end? Why would I create such a world? Time and again I kept coming back to the enigma of the disappearance of Charlie

Villalobos. Had he existed? Had I made him up? Was I the one that was crazy?

* * *

A week after my last call from Charlie Villalobos, I sat in my office at the end of a long day of counseling and tried to collect my thoughts. I still had found no external evidence to support the fact that Charlie Villalobos ever existed. I had attended the screening of Choo Choo's film, and there was Choo Choo as big, energetic and smiling as ever. As always, even at a premiere, with camera in hand. And with him that night was the special star of his movie. Choo Choo had managed to get the celebrated actress, Julia Miranda, to star in his film, and this had guaranteed worldwide distribution. And, of course, everyone in Arroyo Grande came out for the premiere.

After the screening, I took him aside and asked what he had been doing the past few years, the years I knew he had been dead as a doornail! For Christ's sake, I had attended his funeral at the Arroyo Grande cemetery! Choo Choo informed me that after his undergraduate schooling at USC, his undergraduate student film, "Attack of the Lowrider Zombies," had been picked up by Paramount. He had been given the financing to reshoot the film as a major feature. Of course, Julia Miranda was the key factor—studio heads wondered why a name star would star in a low-budget film for free. Unheard of! He had to wait for a year and a half before her schedule freed up, but now the movie was being released worldwide, putting him on the map as an up-and-coming director in Hollywood.

Back in my office, I looked at my watch. Good grief, it was nearly 8 PM! Lupe would be waiting with dinner. As I began to pack up my briefcase, I realized that I was left with two logical possibilities. One option: Charlie Villalobos did exist, did run over and kill Choo Choo Torres, but did so as a figment of someone's dream, and when that dreamer awoke, Charlie ceased to be, and Choo Choo was never really killed—hence explaining his very real presence now. Option two: I made Charlie Villalobos up. And he has never existed and I concocted the whole bizarre story myself, in which case I am crazy nuts. Neither logical explanation was very comforting for me, a psychiatrist.

I turned off the lamps in the office, picked up my briefcase and was about to turn off the main office light when I noticed a glint underneath my desk. I put my briefcase down, walked back to my desk and picked an object up off the floor. When I saw what it was my head reeled. I gasped for air. It was the *illuminated magnifying glass* that Charlie Villalobos had shown me, the one he had picked out of Mrs. Romero's sinkhole! He must have dropped it under my desk on one of his visits.

I took the magnifier and walked over to the office window to examine it more closely. I opened up the curtains and held up the magnifying glass to catch the morning sun shining through the window.

As I perused the simple device, the smile on my face suddenly faded. A terrible realization engulfed me. With dread I looked out the window and realized that the sun was high in the sky. I looked back at the door and saw that my briefcase was still there, where I had left it a minute ago. When it was night time. When I was on my way home. With a fear worse than anything I had ever experienced, I forced myself to look at my watch. It was eleven o'clock in the morning. I had just blacked out the entire night! Could this be happening to me? And then my own words came back to haunt me. You have a choice, I had told Charlie, you have a choice.

RETURN TO ARROYO

I.

Mrs. Romero had been dead for fifteen years, two months, nine days, thirteen hours and fifteen minutes when she awakened to find herself sitting in her favorite rocking chair on the familiar porch of the home she had lived in for more than fifty-five years at 410 Calle Cuatro in Arroyo Grande, Texas. She brought the rocker to an abrupt halt as she looked down at her corpulent body, draped in a pastel print dress and accentuated with a fake pearl necklace and sturdy black leather shoes. She raised her right hand to her face to feel it, then with both hands she felt her ample midriff, as if trying to convince herself that she was indeed sitting in the rocker and alive once again.

"*¡Va!*" she said out loud.

Slowly she raised her considerable self from the rocking chair and made her way to the top of the porch steps. She stopped there and took in the view. The perennially green lawn, that she had worked so hard to keep cut and manicured throughout her lifetime, was now bone dry, overgrown with knee-high, brittle, yellowed grass. A broken realtor sign lay half buried in the debris: "Condemned Property—Do Not Enter!"

She instinctively turned her eyes to a place in the front lawn where many years before a mysterious sinkhole had appeared, an ever-expanding cavity that had subsequently transformed her life and that of so many of Arroyo Grande's citizens.

Now, the vestige of the hole was obscured by the tall parched grass. She noted that beyond the trashed realtor sign, her beautiful white picket fence had been torn down and replaced with a chain-link fence that completely surrounded her property. Outside the gate, on the sidewalk, was a large heap of accumulated trash.

The sight of her transformed home was almost as shocking as her coming to life fifteen years after dying at age 86.

Once again she said to herself, "*¡Va!*"

She ambled her generous weight down the steps and onto the cracked cement walkway that led to the sidewalk in front of her home. As she walked toward the chain-link fence she muttered to herself, "*Mira no más*, if it's not one thing, *pos* it's another!"

When she reached the gate at the chain-link fence, she stopped and wondered how she would get through it. The gate had a large padlock on it. She reached out her hand to gingerly test the lock and found that her hand slipped easily through the wire links as a hot knife might go through butter. She appeared to be transparent.

"*¿Ahora qué?*" she asked herself. "I'm a ghost?"

She pondered this possibility for a moment. And then, with the effervescent aplomb that had distinguished her life and manners for so many years, she said to herself, "*Pos, entonces . . .*"

Without hesitation she walked through the fence, her corpulent body melding through the wire links, and proceeded to march down the sidewalk toward downtown Arroyo Grande. Now and then she'd stop to take in the "Condemned Property" signs posted on each house along the block. At each house, she'd comment to herself, with the solemnity of a religious incantation, "¡*Dios mío*¡ If it's not one thing, *pos* it's another!"

* * *

At that moment, 240,000 miles above Mrs. Romero, on the surface of the moon, Reymundo Salazar stood in the shadow of the Alpine Ridge. To the Northeast he could make out the rim of crater Aristotle and to the South the jagged peaks of the Caucasus Mountains. Years before his induction as the youngest astronaut in the training program at the Houston Space Center, Reymundo had been the star pitcher for the Arroyo Grande Sluggers baseball team. More than once he had hit homeruns clear out of the ballpark at Jefferson High School. Now he was preparing to do himself one better.

Reymundo had found a mound of moondust ten inches above the surrounding terrain and had carefully brushed away a pitcher's rubber plate on it. He then paced off sixty feet six inches to where he outlined a five-sided area measuring 17 inches square—the batter's home plate. From his airtight astronaut suit, he pulled out two items. One was a piece of hyperlight titanium alloy cylinder that measured 3 inches in circumference and a tapered foot long. He unscrewed the lower end of the cylinder and drew from within it another piece of titanium alloy which extended another foot, and within that he pulled out yet another extension, also measuring a foot. The last piece he pulled out measured six inches in length.

The metal pieces screwed into each other, leaving Reymundo holding what was unmistakably a baseball bat measuring the National League required 3 and ½ feet in length. Close inspection of the alloy would reveal that it was comprised of microscopic particles of an advanced balsa wood compound, legally meeting major league specifications that the bat be "made of wood." He tried a couple of practice swings with the newly assembled bat. He was careful not to overdo it, lest the momentum of his swing carry his body off the surface of the airless, low-gravity moon.

Next he pulled out a collapsed cocoon made of microsynthetic mylar.

He released a catch on the surface of the cocoon and it instantly popped open, expanding into the familiar spherically shaped baseball orb he had played with for so many years in his youth. This particular baseball was unique, however, in that it was made of mylar panels which looked very much like tiny wind sails. Indeed, what he held in his hand was nothing less than a tiny solar sail vehicle construed in the shape of a baseball. Reymundo tossed the ball to his astronaut friend and copilot of this lunar mission, Jim Henderson.

"You ready?" Jim asked over the intercom.

"Let's make history!" Reymundo replied.

Jim Henderson reared back in familiar pitcher stance, his right hand holding the ball, his head turned down. "Babe Ruth," Henderson said under his breath, "Eat your heart out!" With that he pitched the ball to Reymundo.

Time seemed to slow down as the mylar-covered ball floated toward Reymundo. Finally, and it did seem like an eternity for Reymundo, the ball neared within striking distance. With one carefully measured swing, Reymundo's bat connected with the ball, sending it spinning off the surface of the moon and into the vacuum of space.

Reymundo and Jim stood in awe as the tiny ball floated silently into the abyss above them.

"With those solar panels, that baby is going to leave the solar system in twenty years!" Jim said. "And partner, you'll have made history. The first baseball ball to be batted out of the solar system!"

"By my calculations," Reymundo replied, "it'll actually be twenty-two years, but who's counting?

Later, back in the cockpit of the lunar module, Reymundo and Jim prepared for the liftoff that would take them back to earth orbit, where they would announce their record-setting feat back home to NASA and JPL colleagues, and, of course, the National Baseball League.

Henderson was systematically going through the countdown of system functions. Reymundo, sitting next to him, was confirming each system check with a "go," when he detected an unmistakable presence behind him. He turned in his seat and was shocked to see a face that it took him a moment to recognize. Could it be? Yes! A face he hadn't seen in years. It was Mrs. Romero from Arroyo Grande!

The elderly woman leaned in and whispered into Reymundo's ear. "We need you back home," she said. Then the apparition was instantly gone.

"What you'd say?" Henderson inquired.

"Huh" replied Reymundo, his eyes still locked onto the space where Mrs. Romero had just been.

"Did you say something?"

"No, nothing," Reymundo replied, still trying to make sense of what had just happened. "Nothing at all."

* * *

Junior Valdez had just completed his final session for the afternoon at his office on Calle Dos, across the street from the Old Town Plaza. It was six months since he had reopened his practice after his brief but intense psychotic episode. With a clean bill of health, he was now able to once again offer aid to others. He was happy that fifteen-year-old Becky Chávez was making progress after several weeks of therapy and a prescription for Fluoxetine. When her parents brought her in with severe depression, it didn't take long for him to diagnose Becky's sleep problems and her frequent absences after meals as telltale signs of *bulimia nervosa.* He was putting away his notes when the light on his desk suddenly went on. The light signaled when someone had entered his waiting room.

"Hmm," he said to himself, "who could that be?"

He was sure he was through with patients for the day, unless someone had mistaken an appointment time, which now and then happened.

He walked to the door and opened it.

Before him stood an elderly lady that his reason told him could not be. He knew this for a fact, because he had been a pallbearer at her funeral fifteen years earlier. Junior was speechless as his mind raced to explain the presence of this long dead *anciana* before him,

"Mrs. Romero?" he asked tentatively, still in disbelief.

The aged woman smiled and nodded.

Junior Valdez was dumbfounded. His analytical, no-nonsense mind demanded an answer to this mystery. He asked himself, how can I be seeing a woman who has been dead for years? I need more objectively verifiable data, he thought to himself, to determine whether I am hallucinating—not again!—or whether there is some scientific explanation for this phenomenon. A hologram?

"Come in, come in," Junior Valdez said, opening the door into his office wider and turning to usher her in.

With his back turned, he heard the woman's voice behind him: "M'*ijo*, put your fancy psychiatry aside for a moment and realize you're needed at the city council."

Junior turned around to ask why and discovered he stood in the outer waiting room alone. The woman had disappeared.

He stared at the empty space where she had stood only a moment earlier. He thought to himself, so much for objectively verifiable data.

* * *

Meanwhile, three blocks over, at the Maldonado Brothers auto shop on Calle Cinco, Raúl and Simón Maldonado were trying to make sense out of a notice they had received from the City Bureau of Planning that had been buried on a desk for weeks under a stack of *Motor Trend* magazines. When Raúl finally noticed and opened the correspondence, he read that the property the brothers leased from Don Carlos Vásquez, a local landowner and entrepreneur, was up for condemnation by right of eminent domain.

"I don't get it," said Raúl, "can they do that? Just condemn this property right out from under us? We've been here for twenty years!"

"That's what it says right here," Simón acknowledged. "Says there's going to be a public hearing on . . . heck, that's tomorrow!"

"Well, we're going to see about this!" Raúl said indignantly. "Those *cabrones* aren't going to kick us out of our shop!"

Just then, Mrs. Romero walked past the open-gated entrance to the auto body shop. She paused for a moment and turned to wave at the two brothers.

"*¡No se les olvide!*" she called out. "The public hearing!"

Raúl and Simón were so shocked by the apparition that they didn't say a word. Mrs. Romero turned and continued on her way downtown. She was soon gone from sight. The two brothers looked at each other in disbelief.

"Was that really . . . ?" Simón asked.

"Damn, it sure looked like her."

"What the hell'd she say?"

"The public hearing. I guess she wants us to show up."

"We damn well will!"

* * *

Throughout that afternoon, Señora Romero appeared to her friends in Arroyo Grande in various ways. At her store, Mesquite Books, Terri Butler found an old woman sitting quietly in the classics section pouring over a copy of Rudy Anaya's *Bless Me Ultima.*

"May I help you?" Terri offered.

The woman turned and Terri instantly recognized a face she had known for years. It took only a moment for Terri to process what her senses were telling her—Terri was a very smart person.

"Mrs. Romero? How can it be you?"

"It can and is, Terri," the woman replied. "I'm not sure how it happened. I thought I had died. But here I am. *¡Va!* Anyway, listen. It's Arroyo Grande that may soon be dead unless we do something about it."

"You mean the hearing tomorrow night?"

"Exactly. Terri, Arroyo Grande needs you now."

"What can I do?"

"You'll know when the time comes."

With that, the elderly woman put the book back on the shelf, walked to the door of the bookstore, turned to wave at Terri and then was gone.

* * *

Elsewhere in the universe, at the concrete plaza in front of the Basilica de la Virgen de Guadalupe, on the northern outskirts of Mexico City, Smiley Rojas had just finished performing as lead dancer in the powerful and exhausting "Fire Dance" by the Danzantes Aztecas dance troupe he commanded. The site was where the Basilica had been built in 1536. According to tradition, this was where the Virgin Mary, in the form of the native Indian deity Tonantzín, had appeared to an Indian peasant named Juan Diego Cuahtlatoatzin in 1531 and spoken to him in náhuatl, asking him to have the basilica built there.

The "Fire Dance" symbolically commemorated the Aztec belief that the world came to a fiery end every 52 years and then was renewed by the sun, Tonatiauh, for another 52 years. The dance required Smiley to dance over a lit fire and toast his knees, calves and bare feet in a symbolic representation of the earth's fiery demise and renewal.

Ordinarily Smiley's tough skin endured the flames without mishap, but this time he had overdone it to please the unusually large crowd of tourists. He was rubbing soothing ointment over his toasted skin when he felt a tap on his shoulder. He turned and looked up to see someone standing over him, someone he hadn't seen in years.

"*Ya párale con las danzas, tu gente te necesita en Arroyo Grande.*"

Without another word, Mrs. Romero turned in the direction of the basilica, crossed herself and then disappeared into the crowd of photo-snapping tourists.

* * *

In Los Angeles, California, Frank Del Roble, an editor at the *Los Angeles Times*, found himself strutting into his boss's office on the third floor of the Times building on 1st Street and perfunctorily lectured the managing editor that he was long overdue a break.

"What are you talking about?" the managing editor asked.

"I need time to regroup my creative juices and so I'm taking a month off *with pay*, and I expect you to approve it!" Frank made no mention of a recent encounter he'd had with a female octogenarian in the elevator going up to his office.

"Well, you just can't do that," his editor replied. "I *won't* approve it."

"If you don't like it, you can fire me!" Frank said. With more vehemence than was probably necessary, he turned and left the office.

* * *

Across town, on Stage 8 of the Paramount Studios, where Alfred Hitchcock's *Rear Window* and the *Star Trek Voyager* television series had been filmed, work was at a stand-still after the fourteenth disastrous take of a love scene between Julia Miranda and her newly discovered leading man, Marco Jeffries.

The director of the film went up to Julia and berated her. With great relish, he told her she was a has-been and that, unless she brought something special to the party, she might as well go home! To his shock, Julia replied, "What a splendid idea! That's exactly what I'm going to do. I'm going home to Arroyo Grande, right now! This instant!" With that she returned to her trailer, where she collected her clothing and personal effects and then made her way to her waiting limousine where, to her surprise, she discovered an elderly lady seated in the back seat waiting for her. The two women smiled warmly at one another.

"To LAX," Julia said to her driver.

"And step on it!" Mrs. Romero added.

* * *

Father Ronquillo opened the door to the rectory office at the San Fernando Cathedral in downtown San Antonio and welcomed in the two auxiliary bishops of the San Antonio Archdiocese. Five years earlier, Father Ronquillo had been elevated to archbishop of the sprawling Archdiocese that encompassed 139 parishes located in Texas cities as far west as Del Rio, as far north as Kerrville, as far east as Gonzalez and as far south as Pleasanton. Earlier that morning, as Father Ronquillo prepared for the six o'clock mass, he had been visited by an old friend, and that had prompted him to call together his two loyal auxiliary archbishops.

"Please sit down, brothers," he said, indicating the padded chairs in his office. "I need to attend to some unfinished business at my old parish in Arroyo Grande, and I'm going to need you both to oversee the archdiocese while I'm gone."

"Yes, of course, your excellency," Archbishop O'Flynn said.

"Your excellency," Archbishop Contreras asked, "how long will you be gone?"

"Not really sure, brother. Whatever God wills."

"May we inquire about the purpose of your visit?" Archbishop Contreras asked.

"God has given me a sign. He wants me to go to Arroyo Grande."

"And what will you do there?" Archbishop O'Flynn asked.

"As always, follow God's instructions."

"How long will you be gone?"

"Only God knows. Let us pray, *hermanos*."

* * *

At the third level, South Wing, of the Pirámide construction site in the isolated desert north of Tucson, Arizona, Bobby Hernández was midway through his night shift patrol of the massive edifice. The security patrol was pure fiction since the building site was in full operation twenty-four hours a day and there were so many workers and security people present that it would, indeed, have been quite a challenge for anyone to try any theft, sabotage or other nefarious activity. Since leaving the Arroyo Grande police department three years earlier, after a particularly unsettling incident on a night patrol, Bobby had taken up Jeannie De La Cruz's offer to head the security department at the Pirámide site.

Though it was almost midnight, Bobby looked forward to his "lunch break," when he could share a cup of coffee with his old friends from Arroyo Grande who were also working the night shift: Rudy Vargas, Pete Navarro and Lil' Louie Ruiz. He welcomed these late-night talks with friends because they allowed him to forget the terrible nightmares that had racked him in recent years.

The foursome had gathered under the glare of the huge light towers that illuminated the top tier of the pyramid's third level and were opening up their box lunches and popping open their thermoses, when suddenly Bobby looked up to the night sky and beheld a sight that forced him to gag on his coffee.

"Look!" he sputtered.

The others in the group followed his gaze and one by one, their mouths fell open and they slowly rose to their feet, transfixed by the sight before them. Descending from the sky, silhouetted and backlit by the light towers, was a corpulent human figure descending as if lowered by an invisible cable. Bobby's first thought was that they were being blessed with a holy apparition.

"It's the *Virgen de Guadalupe!*" Bobby cried out.

As the apparition got closer, however, the lower track lights on the roof revealed the chubby figure not to be a deity at all but rather someone they well remembered from their childhood.

"I wanted to get your attention," Mrs. Romero explained, hanging in the air above them. "And I wanted you all to see me together, so you'll know you're not dreaming and that I'm not kidding around!"

The four men were speechless.

"*Muchachos*, you're all needed back in Arroyo Grande. You get moving tomorrow and don't give Jeannie any lip!"

And then, as if she were made of some magical confetti, the figure exploded into a million tiny particles of light that soon disappeared into the night.

The four men looked at each other in amazement.

"Was that . . . ?" Pete Navarro offered.

"Had to be," said Lil' Louie Ruiz.

Just then, the men heard the door of the cage elevator that carried people to the top of the construction site open. Jeannie de la Cruz stepped out of the elevator and walked toward them. "Hi, guys," she called out, "I have something important to tell you. It's about tomorrow."

But before Jeannie could continue, Rudy Vargas, who was never much for protocol, picked up his thermos and lunch bucket and turned to his friends. "I think we're done for the night, *vatos*. I'll do the driving tomorrow. If we leave by seven in the morning, we should hit Arroyo Grande by mid-afternoon."

Jeannie didn't say a word, just nodded to herself.

* * *

And so, the next day they started arriving. From as close by as El Paso, Las Cruces and Tucson, and as far away as Los Angeles, New York, Mexico City, Tokyo and Paris. Past citizens of Arroyo Grande who had been gone a day, a month, a year or a decade and were now driven by a profound need to return to what once had been their home. Some thought they had come to this conclusion on their own, while others were troubled by an unexplainable, close encounter of an unpredictable and thoroughly unsettling kind.

II.

So check this out. I'm sitting in the cramped middle seat between a mother with a squalling baby and a two hundred and fifty pound football player on the interminable plane ride from Los Angeles to El Paso. This is a 750-mile trip that takes two and half hours. But the equally painful bus ride from the El Paso airport to Arroyo Grande, which is only 60 miles, *also* takes about two and half hours. I ask myself, how does that work? Well, the damn bus stops in Ysleta, Socorro, San Elizario, Fabens and Fort Hancock, with 15 minute waits at each stop. We finally reach Arroyo Grande two and a half hours later. Go figure.

Imagine my surprise when the long gray dog rolls into the bus depot at Main and 6th Street. Yeah, that's where centuries ago Julia Miranda gave me my first adult kiss, that moment forever burned in my mind. So there, sitting on a bench outside the entrance to where the bus dumps off its human cargo is none other than Mrs. Romero!

Hey, surprise is an understatement. You see, she's been dead for what . . . fourteen, fifteen years? I attended her funeral and placed a rose on her coffin. So why and how and what is she doing sitting on this bench outside the bus depot, alive as all get-out? And, if I may, looking pretty damn good for being dead for fifteen years. I grab my duffle bag, camera in hand, quickly leap down the steps of the bus and go right up to her. I'm not afraid! But before I can utter a single word, she looks up at me and says, "Waiting for you, Choo Choo."

I'm thinking, what?

"Señora Romero, is this really you?"

"Pos, ¿a quién esperabas?"

Now, mentally, I'm checking my pulse, pinching my arm, and slapping myself on the face. Am I dreaming? What is this?

"No, you're not dreaming, *m'ijo*," she says.

What? Is she reading my mind?

"In a way, Choo Choo," she says. "I'm here to tell you that there is a very important meeting of the city council tonight. They are going to vote on a plan to completely destroy *las casitas del barrio*. Not just my poor *casa* but that of your parents as well! You have to stop them!"

Hey, I hear you. It's what's brought me back to Arroyo Grande in the first place. My dad called a few weeks back and read the city notice that the house my parents had bought on Calle Cuatro was being condemned. We'd moved there from the apartment complex we lived in at Calle Diez in my freshman year at Jefferson High. The notice had said it was by right of eminent domain and that each property owner would be satisfactorily compensated. Yeah, right. The notice said there'd be a hearing in a few weeks.

"This is our home, Choo Choo," my dad had said over the phone. "We don't want no compensation and we don't want to move. Isn't there anything we can do?"

"I'll come home and we'll testify at that meeting," I told him.

Later, I got a surprise call from Yoli Mendoza in New York saying she was coming home for the same reason: her parent's home was on the chopping block. I'm wondering if she's arrived in Arroyo Grande yet.

"Yes," Mrs. Romero says. She really *is* reading my mind. "She's here. Yoli arrived yesterday, *m'ijo*. She's busy now, but she'll be there tonight."

Just then I see another sight I haven't seen in years. Don Sebastiano Diamante and his little dog Peanuts. Both of them ambling down the sidewalk toward me and Mrs. Romero. And I know that both of them are long dead as well. Peanuts many, many years ago, and Don Sebastiano just two days before Mrs. Romero passed away. Everyone said *she* died of a broken heart. They buried them together.

"Choo Choo!" he calls out. "*And if ye go to war in your land against the enemy that oppresseth you, then ye shall blow an alarm with the trumpets*, Numbers 10, 9."

Then he turns to Mrs. Romero. "*Mi princesa azteca*, are you finished with your work yet?"

"Not yet, *mi querido Don Quijote*. Just a few more."

"A few more?" I ask, trying to make sense of it all.

"You think you're the only who has forgotten about your barrio and needs to be reminded there's work to be done? *Anda, vete*, and make sure you stop that city council from destroying our community!"

I walk away in a daze. Is this really happening? I turn to look back and make sure I have really seen Mrs. Romero, and sure enough she and Don Sabastiano are sitting side by side on the depot bench, laughing at something she's said. Little Peanuts rests comfortably on his master's lap. Just like when they were all alive.

* * *

¡Híjole! Sometimes I wish I could do everything myself. I hate to depend on other people! Don't they always screw things up? Just leave it to Yoli and I'll get things done!

Case in point. It's five minutes to seven on the night the Arroyo Grande City Council is set to vote final approval for the plan to raze the barrio from 1st to 6th Street, and from Pershing Avenue to La Loma. It's a plan devised by that nefarious team of Harold Rebber and Jonathan Barrón so they can complete the expansion of the convention center and tourism complex they have been discreetly devising for years. So where was my back-up?

Choo Choo, *para empezar!* He promised he would be here do or die, and where is he? Probably still back at USC humping some California golden girl. And my old friend Max Martínez. Max whom I could always depend on! Also MIA. Ay, Maximiliano, why are you letting me down? And Jeannie de la Cruz. She said she'd be here for sure. And that she'd bring the whole gang from that crazy pyramid project of hers—Bobby Hernández, Rudy Vargas, Louie Ruiz and the others. Where are they? I told them to get here an hour before the seven o'clock meeting of the council.

All of them are no shows. And what about the city council itself, eh? Five minutes before showtime and not one alderman is seated yet! In fact, besides a few staffers, I'm the only person in the council chambers. Wait a minute . . . I look at my watch again and then suddenly stop.

Oops!

¡Qué menso! I start feeling really, really dumb. Yes, my watch says five of seven. But when I flew into El Paso the day before, I forgot to change it from New York time. I'm two hours off! No one's here because it isn't even six yet! It's barely five o'clock local time.

Sure enough, an hour later, right on schedule, everyone starts showing up. The Maldonado brothers, Max Martínez, Terri Butler, Howard Meltzer, Harry Gamboa, the band members of the Nuevas Calaveras and their families, Mrs. Tanguma, Doña Cuca, Mrs. Ybarra, the Man with No Name, Junior Valdez, the Domínguez twins and their families, even Archbishop Ronquillo! And who's that strutting in? It's that *pachu-*

co guy that dogged Rudy and María Vargas for so long! It's like a darn family reunion!

And of course, Jeannie and her whole gang who have driven in from their Pyramid project in Arizona also show up. Yes, even the celebrities: Mr. Youngest-Astronaut-in-History himself, Reymundo Salazar, and Pulitzer-prize-winning journalist, Frank Del Roble, and, of course, the grand dame of them all, Julia Miranda, star of stage and screen. I can tell she's arrived because of the paparazzi that precede her entrance into the city council chambers. Oh boy, everyone wants an autograph. Celebrities . . . ugh! But where the heck is Choo Choo?

"Yoli!"

I turn and there he is. Big smile, a little sun-tanned, and, of course, his ever-present camera in hand.

I go over and give him a big sloppy one on the lips.

"Choo Choo, you're here," I say to him. "You ARE my dreamboat."

I think he's a little taken aback by the big one I planted on his lips. But he sure isn't complaining. Then he turns conspiratorial. "Fill me in, Yoli. What the hell is going on anyway?"

* * *

I think of myself as a pretty good reporter. But before I moved to the *Los Angeles Times*, during my tenure at the *Arroyo Grande Gazette*, I managed to miss what would become the biggest story in Arroyo Grande. Right under my nose! Not till I did some fact-checking at the *LA Times* archives and made a few phone calls did the whole picture suddenly come into focus.

Harold Rebber and Jonathan Barrón planned it all pretty well. First they mapped out a portion of Arroyo Grande that runs from Calle Uno north to Calle Seis and from Sycamore

Street, past Mercado and on to La Loma. It's a rectangular chunk of the old city that encompasses a dozen city blocks where the poor people live. Its elevation is lower than the rest of Arroyo Grande, people sometimes call it "El Hoyo." Rebber and Barrón bought up bank loans and started to foreclose on those who couldn't make their monthlies. It only took them a couple of years and they've got a dozen homes vacated. They declared the homes uninhabitable and they got their cronies on the city council to approve condemnation of the homes.

Of course, they carefully avoided anything East of Sycamore, places that would be a problem, like St. Anthony's parish, Thomas Jefferson High School, the historic Old Town Plaza and, of course, City Hall Square.

I should have known something was up when they cleverly established a beachhead a few years ago with the Skyscraper that Flew on Calle Cinco between Sycamore and Mercado. Like devious military generals orchestrating a pincer move, they'll now connect the newly completed convention center at 1st Street and Main and expand it into the new occupied territory, linking it all to the Skyscraper that Flew down on Calle Cinco. It's a masterful blitzkrieg of territorial occupation that in one fell swoop gives Rebber and Barrón complete ownership of a quarter of Arroyo Grande and control of much of the rest. No Walmart or Target could have devised it better.

All they need now is for the city council to approve their petition to declare the remaining homes in the twelve-block area condemned by right of eminent domain—the greater good for the greater number of people. Rebber and Barrón will create the largest Casino and Resort complex in the state of Texas and make a fortune. Humph, eminent domain!

* * *

It scares me to think of what might happen, because, I know. *I've lived it*. While the idea of Rebber and Barrón taking over the town and converting it into a giant casino may seem like a mighty, mighty exaggeration to some people in Arroyo Grande, I know that it *really can* happen.

In spite of the recovery from what the doctor described as my false memory, I can't forget the visceral feeling of being there. I can still hear Choo Choo cursing at the blackjack dealers like he owned us. And Yoli! Not the Yoli I know now, but the Yoli that was transformed into a narcissistic, belligerent and cruel demon. I can still see all of us grasping for whatever scraps Rebber and Barrón would throw our way, while we did each other in without regard to our old friendships or just plain human decency. That's why we have to stop them! My hand reaches out to clasp Gale's, sitting next to me in the city council chamber. Yoli says that she, Max Martínez and Mayor Cervantes have come up with a plan. Whatever it is, I sure as hell hope it works!

* * *

In spite of all the intrigue, it's really pretty simple. Mayor Cervantes is the only one on this damn city council with—what's the expression in Spanish?—*huevos*! That's it . . . or, I guess in her case, it would be . . . ovaries. I know this because of how she defended me when they tried to close down Mesquite Books because I was behind on my city license permits. Hey, I lost the paperwork! That doesn't mean they can take away my livelihood! Nancy stood up for me. "Don't you worry, Terri," she said, "I'll handle this!" Now she's the only person on the city council who can see what they've done and intend to do to this barrio and the only one who can stop them dead in their tracks!

Ed Carrillo, Al Synder and Alfonso Sainz are all in the pockets of Rebber and Barrón. Johnnie Wilson, Mary García and Henry Ponce are so wishy-washy they'll go with whichever way the side they think is winning.

Look at these smug creeps filing in. As they take their seats I can see they're really nervous as hell. And well they should be. I bet they've not seen this kind of community turnout for a city council meeting in years!

And look at all our folks in the audience. Heck, it's the who's-who of Arroyo Grande, past and present. People I haven't seen for so long! Why, that's Frank Del Roble over there, from the *Los Angeles Times*, please! And there's all those youngsters from Calle Cuatro and Calle Cinco—Choo Choo, Bobby Hernández, Reymundo Salazar, Jeannie de la Cruz and Junior Valdez. How many times have they come to the Mesquite looking for a book on this or that? And now, all of them grown up and professionals in so many different fields. And some of them . . . Oh, my god! Julia Miranda is here! How the heck did she even hear about this?

Look, here come the two major creeps themselves, Rebber and Barrón.

* * *

"Good Lord, Harold, where'd all these people come from?"

"Don't you worry none, Jonathan. Carrillo, Sainz and Snyder know what they have to do if they want to get what we talked about."

"Let's hope they can bring the others along."

"That's their job, Jonathan, that's their job."

* * *

Nancy's got to win over those worthless undecideds, simple as that. If they vote against Rebber and Barrón, then Nancy can be the deciding vote, the tie-breaker. I may not be a political analyst, but I know how to fix things. They don't call me Max the Fixer-Upper for nothing. But hey, it doesn't take an Einstein to do the math.

Three aldermen in the pockets of Rebber and Barrón—doubtless they'll benefit personally from the new Casino and Sports Complex and attendant hotel, market place and entertainment center. Then there are the three wishy-washy nincompoops who'd sell their grandmothers down the river if it meant they'd make an extra buck. So fearless Nancy has got to win over those three gutless wonders. Fortunately, ole Max Martínez has a thing or two up his sleeve. Yes sir, that I do!

* * *

"*Viejo*, I don't think they can see us anymore."

"But *mi azteca*, they could see us quite well earlier in the day. *¿Qúe pasó?*"

"Choo Choo nearly stepped on me when he came into the Council chambers. I spoke to Yoli this morning and now she sees right through me. *Se me hace que* we're invisible to them, *viejo*."

"Invisible?"

"It would make sense. They're so caught up in the struggle that they've forgotten we're the ones who got them here. *¿Qué no?*"

"Seems disrespectful!"

"Not at all, *viejo*. We mustn't take it personally. *Ya no nos necesitan*. We got them here. Now it's up to them."

"I think Peanuts has to pee."

"Well take him outside. I want to sit a bit and see what they have up their sleeves."

* * *

"Mayor Cervantes, are you telling this council we will have to listen to all of the people on this list before we vote on the issue at hand?" The look on the face of Ed Carilllo is priceless. He's positively fuming!

"Alderman Carrillo," I reply, "the people on this list have followed the protocol that the council has established. I believe it's Charter Amendment Number 34." I glance at the audience—they're beaming. Of course, I have to make a big deal of reading the citation in question: "Individuals wishing to be heard on any council item to be discussed in a public forum may speak for a period not to exceed ten minutes provided that they register as a speaker with the council's agenda manager within twelve hours of the relevant public hearing."

I can see Al Snyder and Alfonso Sainz are also really pissed.

"Look, there's gotta be more than 250 people on this list! And why didn't the city council hear about these speakers earlier?"

"Actually," I correct him, "there are 263 speakers by last count before I called the session into order. The 263 people who have signed up to speak did so within the last twelve hours, as attested to by their representative and notary public Maximilian Martínez. After that, no more people can be registered to speak. And the earliest moment to inform the council, since people started signing up only two hours ago, was just now when I told you."

"How can we listen to all of these people in one night?"

"Why, Alderman Sainz," I reply in all seriousness, "I don't believe we can. We'll have to continue the hearing on the proposed condemnation of properties in Arroyo Grande until all the pros and cons are heard. We certainly wouldn't want to arbitrarily veto the proposal put forth by Mr. Harold Rebber and Mr. Jonathan Barrón without having heard all of the good reasons why they should be allowed to proceed. And doubtless there may be a voice or two in the audience speaking to the contrary."

The whole room erupts in laughter at that.

"But," I continue, "they all deserve to be heard." Damn, I'm having so much fun sticking it to these hypocritical, self-serving cretins!

"A continuation of the motion? Well, how long will that take?"

"Let me see . . . ," I say, savoring the moment, "each person is entitled to a full ten minutes, by city ordinance. I expect most of these citizens will want to avail themselves of their full ten minutes. So that's 263 times ten minutes, that's 2630 minutes divided by sixty minutes per hour, comes out to about 48 hours of testimony, give or take an hour. Since each city council meeting, by charter, must adjourn three hours after first gavel, I guess we're going to have to continue this motion by Rebber and Barrón for the next fourteen weeks, give or take a week."

"Outrageous!" Carrillo yells. "This is preposterous!"

From the front row Harold Rebber rises and calls out to Carrillo, "You can't let them do this. We need that okay tonight. We've got bulldozers waiting!"

Jonathan Barrón glares at Alderman Sainz, "We talked about this!"

What follows is general bedlam as the council members argue with one another and the audience. I expected this would happen when Max Martínez first approached me with the idea a few weeks ago. Damn that Max, he's smart! He'd seen the Rebber-Barrón move coming way before I had seen it. He had concluded that unless we did something drastic, the city council would ram through the permit. That's when he called me with his ingenious plan to block the voting. I was only too eager to help out!

"We'll hear from the first of our speakers," I announce, banging on my gavel and getting things back to order. "Mr. Raúl Maldonado and Mr. Simón Maldonado, representing the small businesses on Calle Cinco. Gentlemen, you may step up to the microphone."

* * *

This city council meeting reminds me of reporting on Mrs. Romero's sinkhole for the *Gazette*. I remember all the people who were there at Mrs. Romero's that day and, lo and behold, I see most of them here today. The first speakers have been pretty good, full of anger and passion. The Maldonado brothers talking about the twenty years of service they have given to the community and how the new casino will destroy their clientele. That's right, hit them on the casino. Let's call this eminent domain bullshit for what it is: a land grab by Rebber and Barrón so they can build their damn casino complex!

Junior Valdez reminds everyone of how important his dad's store was for a whole generation of barrio residents before the Supermart opened up. Terri Butler on how the proposed casino complex poses a moral question: Is gambling at the casino the example we want to set for the youth of Arroyo Grande? And Archbishop Ronquillo, who's come all the way from San Antonio, bringing that Catholic authority to it all. Heck, I should pitch a story just on him to the *Times*!

And then the local homeowners. Choo Choo speaking on behalf of his mom and dad—the reference to the medals his father won while defending our country was genius! And now, after defending his country, he and his family are being thrown out in the street. Count on Choo Choo for hyperbole! Yoli with her mother and father at her side, speaking for all of the residents of the homes up for destruction. Wow, what a show! Makes me want to be back here with the people I love. Gee, I wonder what Gloria would say about leaving Los Angeles?

* * *

"Mr. Chicas Patas," I say, speaking into the mike. "I'm afraid you're at the end of your ten minutes." I wonder if anyone understood what the heck he was saying. Not like any Spanish I learned at school.

"*No hay de qué, su honorífica. ¡Todo tirile! ¡Planchao y firme! Ya aflojo con el Mike. Y sabes, me caen guangos estos rucos tapaos. En otras palabras, 'pa los mensos,'* you just can't let these *sinvergüenzas* take our barrio away from us!"

There's an applause from the standing-room-only crowd as Mr. Chicas Patas sits down. I turn to the other council members. "I see that our meeting time is up as well. That concludes today's public speakers. We've heard from 16 of the speakers." I continue, smiling at each of my colleagues, "we'll resume the speakers at next week's council meeting." And, of course, I can't help getting a dig in: "Only 247 speakers left to go!"

Harold Rebber and Jonathan Barrón left after the first speakers. They were fuming. But the members of the city council had to sit through all of the speakers. I caught Carrillo and Sainz both dozing off more than once. I expect they'll come back next week with some devious proposal to sidebar the speakers. But we'll be ready. I can see from the faces of the crowd that we're all in it for the long haul.

* * *

We've stopped Rebber and Barrón dead in their tracks! Well, at least for now. I'm so proud of my people. Thank you, Lord, for helping us out. As we file out of the council chambers, it occurs to me that I haven't seen many of these folks since I left Arroyo Grande to take up residence in San Antonio. I can't help but remember the many times I would see the Arroyo Grande sluggers practicing on my morning run, all the great potential I saw in each of them.

And they have not disappointed me. Choo Choo, Yoli, Reymundo, Junior Valdez, Bobby, the Domínguez twins, look how they've turned out! Now here we all are once again. I can think of no better way to celebrate than to have a grand party. And yes, this would certainly be celebrating the Lord's work. For who else but the Lord could have brought us all together? Why, I'm going to tap into the San Antonio Archdiocese's discretionary fund to pay for whatever it takes for St. Anthony's to host the biggest party that Arroyo Grande has ever seen. I nudge Father O'Keefe, who now presides over St. Anthony's parish. "Father, we have some work to do."

"Hermanos y hermanas," I call out to the crowd, "the Archdiocese of San Antonio would like to celebrate this moment of God's victory with a barbecue party at St. Anthony's, and you're all invited!"

Well, that's all it takes.

The Maldonado Brothers and their wives, Bibi and Lupe, who are renowned for their out-of-this world fajitas and tri-tip barbecue, immediately volunteer to do the cooking. Rudy Vargas, Lil Louie Ruiz and David Sandoval offer to get the refreshments. And Yoli Mendoza and Choo Choo Torres, with the help of the boys from the La Loma and Segundo Barrio gangs, will set up the church tables and folding chairs in the parking lot behind St. Anthony's.

As the townspeople start making their way down Calle Nueve to the parish, I look back to the front of City Hall. I don't like what I see. Aldermen Sainz, Carrillo and Snyder are talking quietly on the steps. And they looked deadly serious, mean and conspiratorial. I can see that they're not going to give up without a fight.

III.

"Choo Choo!"

I grab his arm and pull him aside from the crowd of hundreds that have gathered in the parking lot of St. Anthony's church. "Wow! Just look at all of our friends that we haven't seen for years. And here we all are, just like that great sinkhole morning at Mrs. Romero's years go."

"I was thinking of the time we stayed up all night to watch the meteor shower light show on the skyscraper that flew."

"Yes, it's just like that. Here we all are, telling stories, joking and being together once again."

"And you and I," he says.

That stops me. Even after Choo Cho came out to New York to my Sasonz opening so many years ago, we still decided to remain "friends" until the future said otherwise.

"The future is now, Yoli," he says earnestly.

¡Híjole! He's been thinking what I've been thinking.

"It's community," someone says, disrupting the moment.

I turn to see Junior Valdez approaching us with a beer in hand. "It's community," he repeats. I can tell he's really happy. "That's what this is all about. How we all help each other and work toward a goal bigger than all of us!"

"Well, here's to community," Choo Cho says, lifting up the beer he's been holding.

Me? I've been drinking Chardonnay. So I lift up my Styrofoam cup filled with wine (Hey, Styrofoam cups are all they had in the St. Anthony kitchen!). I offer a toast. "Here's to community!"

"Here's to the future," Choo Cho says pointedly.

We all toast. And then I glance across the parking lot and see that Julia Miranda is holding court. *Híjole*, I can't believe I was once jealous of Julia because of Choo Choo's puppy love fixation on her. I wonder what she makes of this whole evening.

* * *

It's so great to be back home among the people I love and that love me. No phony Hollywood agents that can't tell you if they liked your performance because they haven't discussed it yet with their boss at the agency. That's what you really want in life, not an honest opinion, but the tally of a group vote on your performance. Hollywood, ugh!

Here in Arroyo Grande it's real. Real people telling you how they loved me in *Passions of the Heart* but hated my performance in *Sins of the Mother*, and the reasons why. Hey, I long ago developed a hard outer shell and have become immune to criticism. After a while you realize that it's not about your performance but about people wanting to share what they think. People just wanting for you to pay a little attention to them for that brief moment with you. And if you're gracious, as I try to be, you agree with them or somehow make them feel that their comment will somehow make you a better actor. If you're really a good actor, you can pull that off. If you're just a jerk, then you blow off your fans and tell them to go to hell—and diminish them and yourself in the process.

And so here I am at this really great party at St. Anthony's, with people I haven't seen in years, and wanting to spend a few quiet moments with people like Choo Choo Torres, and Max Martínez, missing la señora Romero, and, I'll admit it, even wishing I could see old Miguelito again. I wonder if he's still around?

In the meantime, "Yes, I'd love to sign an autograph for you. Wait a minute, you look familiar. Aren't you . . . ?"

* * *

"I'm Rosalinda Rodríguez," she tells Julia.

Julia explodes with, "Rosalinda, I remember you!" She gives my sweetheart a big hug, "It's so good to see you again!" Julia signs a message and her autograph on a faded lobby card that Rosalinda has saved from the El Paso premiere of *The Wayward Wind*.

Hey, Julia may be a Hollywood superstar but she still has class.

This thing with Rosalinda has really worked out well. I've actually found someone who loves me and whom I love. And we just are so right for each other. For one thing, not only is she cute but she's got brains. When I talk literature or politics, she's right there! "Max," she'll say, "I disagree." And then she'll come up with a really sound argument that makes me rethink my ideas. Wow, I think, how can I be so lucky?

Only thing is, she's really shy. She's so shy that I have to help her do what she really wants to do. "Ay, Max," she tells me earlier in the day, "it's so embarrassing but I would like an autograph from Julia Miranda."

Nothing to be embarrassed about, I tell her. Julia may be a celebrity but she's *puro Arroyo Grande*, she's one of us. Come on, I'll introduce you to her. And now look at the two of them, together just like old friends, even though I'm sure Julia never paid much attention to Rosalinda before. Yep, Julia's a real class act!

* * *

"Mi *princesa azteca*, are we done yet?"

"*¡Cállate, viejo!* Can't you see how much fun I'm having overhearing all these *niños* having a good time?"

"It's past Peanut's bed time."

"Okay, *viejo, ya voy*. But it sure would be nice to talk to all of my friends in person."

"*Corazón*, we're dead. They can't see us anymore."

"No, but I think they know we're here."

* * *

It's getting close to one in the morning, and there seems to be no end to the merriment in the parking lot of St. Anthony's. And I'm patting myself on the back for helping Max get the *gente* out to defend themselves, when suddenly I hear a shout, and here comes Mrs. Quintero, the city clerk, running toward the crowd. *Ay Dios*, now what?

"They're going through with it!" she shouts as she joins the crowd. "The city council has been in secret session and voted to suspend the rules regarding hearing speakers on this issue. Instead, they voted to approve the building permits and they gave a green light to the new Rebber and Barrón development!"

"What, they can't do that!" Nancy Cervantes says. "I'm the mayor!"

"Can and did, Mayor," Mrs. Quintero says. "They passed an emergency motion to do what they wanted to do all along."

"Can they just do that?" I ask.

"Yoli, they can do anything they want," Mrs. Quintero replies, making no effort to hide her disgust. By now the crowd around us has grown.

"Sainz asked if it was legal," she goes on. "Carrillo said it doesn't matter. If people want to stop it, they have to get a restraining order from the court. By the time anybody can do that, the houses will be demolished. After that it won't make any difference whether it was done legally or not. The demolition begins tomorrow morning as planned."

I can't believe my ears. They've pulled a fast one on us and now all of our efforts are dead in the water. I looked over at Choo-Choo. He's doing that nervous thing he does, pushing his glasses back on his nose. I can see he's really getting pissed.

Throughout the crowd people start crying, and arguing and ranting. This is not good. We have to figure out a way to fight back. Then Choo Choo let's out a "No!" at the top of his lungs. He jumps up on the hood of the 1949 Chevy that Rudy Vargas and his friends had pulled from the sinkhole and shouts to all the people present. "We must stop the bulldozers! We must be there tomorrow morning to stop the bulldozers! All of us together!"

IV.

Dawn. The next morning. I'm on the knoll at the south end of the Arroyo Grande cemetery just inside the front gate, across the street from the weathered apartment complex with the "Condemned" sign on it where I grew up. This is where I fell in love with Julia Miranda, and later Yoli Mendoza. From here I can see the entire town stretching out below me.

Off to my left the sun rises over the flat Texas desert—I can see Highway 10 snaking out to Balmorhea, Fort Stockton, Ozona and eventually San Antonio. At the corner of La Loma and Calle Cuatro, the bulldozers are parked, just a few yards from Mrs. Romero's boarded-up house. The block between Mercado and La Loma, Calle Cuatro and Calle Tres is the first city block that Rebber and Barrón have cleared of residents. An entire city block of empty, condemned houses ready for demolition. This is where the decisive battle will take place.

* * *

I run out of the house, down the steps and start out to Calle Cuatro.

Dad calls out after me. "Yoli, your mom and I will catch up with you in a few minutes!"

Hell dad, I think to myself, the whole damn town will be out there this morning. As I walk along, I can feel the tube of xenosium jiggling in my jeans pocket. I've decided that since I'm not ever going to use this gift from Mrs. Romero's sinkhole, that I'll return it. Maybe bury it in the same hole from where it came. Oh look, the crowd is already gathering!

* * *

Gotta get that crack in the patrol car window fixed. I touch it with my finger—it's a small crack, but it'll get bigger. Like the crowd I'm seeing across the street. I don't like it one bit. I've been counting since they started arriving an hour ago. There must be two hundred people here, and more joining up by the minute! A crowd that size can go crazy. This could turn into a riot. But we're prepared.

After the city council meeting last night, I got the call from Alderman Carrillo. "Captain Bowers. The city council has approved the demolition. But we're expecting trouble. Are you and your men up to it?"

I assured the alderman that I will have things under control. Next, I called Chief of Police Higgins in El Paso. Once I explained the situation, he agrees to send in some of his troopers to help me keep the peace. They're riot trained. We'll be ready for whatever happens.

* * *

It wasn't easy convincing Father O'Keefe that we had to stand with the people.

"It's not fitting," he told me, "that the archbishop be part of a public demonstration, be seen with an unruly crowd challenging the authority of the law. Not fitting at all."

Well, I tell him, "Archdiocese or not, I must be with my flock in their time of need. And so must you, Father O'Keefe."

Where's the spine in priests these days? Reluctantly, he agreed, and we prayed together before heading out, seeking God's guidance.

But now that we're here with the protest crowd, I'm frightened. I don't like all those police officers lining up in front of the bulldozers. They're wearing riot gear—that's got to be El Paso police. Arroyo Grande Chief Tom Bowers and his men don't have that kind of gear. Bowers has called for reinforcements, that's what. Help us, Lord. Keep us from harm.

* * *

What's that? Someone's singing, and it seems to be coming from Mrs. Romero's gutted house! It sounds like. Yes, it is! It's a recording, "We Shall Overcome." Wait a minute, I know that voice. It's Pete Seeger! Yes, I think I still have a copy of that album in the Mesquite Book Store record section. I remember filing it away. It's Pete Seeger singing, all right. "We shall overco-o-me . . . " And it's catching on with the crowd.

They're singing along with it now, "We shall overco-o-me, We shall overco-o-me someda-a-a-ay!" Gosh, it brings back memories. Yes, "We shall overcome!"

* * *

"*Mira, mi azteca,* it's our neighbor Juan Alaníz and the Calaveras!"

"*Viejo,* it's the song I remembered they'd be singing in front of our house! *¿Te acuerdas?*"

"You remember this?"

"*Sí, querido,* I remember this moment exactly as we are seeing it."

* * *

Ever since the city council promoted him to Chief of Police, Bowers has been a real jerk. Treats me like I'm his personal assistant instead of a police officer with a year seniority over him. But that makes no difference, he's the Chief now.

"Andy," he tells me over the walkie, "sounds like that music is coming from that corner house over there. Go in and make sure everyone's out of that house. The bulldozers will be starting up in a few minutes."

So I jump over the fence like a trained circus dog and push open the door to the house—Mrs. Romero's house, not that the chief would know. I find the source of the music easy enough—a turntable with speakers attached to an amplifier has been set up at the doorway, with the speakers pointed to where the people are gathering on the street outside. I let the music play on as I inspect the house. If it's transients, I don't want to scare them off before I can arrest them. A few minutes, later I'm done—no vagrants. Whoever set up the turntable is long gone.

I return to the front of the house, take the needle off the record and the music stops. Who has a turn table still in this day and age? I guess that would have been Mrs. Romero before she passed away. I inspect the album cover, some hippy with a banjo. Humph. "Songs of the Civil Rights Movement." I wonder who put this rig together?

* * *

When the crowd sees Andy Armenta emerge from Mrs. Romero's house carrying a turntable and amplifier, they begin to boo him. For a moment I stop playing my *guitarrón* and call out to him, "Andy, don't be a *vendido!*"

Andy glares at me, "Cha Cha Mendiola, you can go to hell." He promptly throws the turntable and speakers over the chain-link fence onto a heap of trash on the sidewalk.

"*Órale, muchachos,*" Juan calls out to us, "it's up to us now! *¡Dale gas!*" I resume playing my worn *guitarrón*, and before long the crowd is singing louder than ever, but now we've changed it into Spanish, "*¡No, no, no nos moverán! ¡No, no, no nos moverán!*"

* * *

I'm busy passing out picket signs to the people in the crowd—wow, must be three hundred people by now. With all the supplies I had at the fix-it shop, it was easy for us to crank these out early this morning. With Choo Choo, Yoli, Jeannie and her wife Gale, Junior, Bobby and the Domínguez Twins, we knocked the signs out in no time at all. And great looking pickets they are: "We Shall Not Be Moved," "Arroyo Grande Forever!" "Down with Rebber and Barrón!"

* * *

I look up and who do I see coming my way but my dear friends Death Dance Domínguez and Louie Díaz, and with them all the kids from the Arroyo Grande Community Youth Services.

"Good to see you, Father Ronquillo!"

"Good to see you boys!"

Within a few moments they're helping me hand out pickets and get the crowd organized—got to say, it's a lot better seeing these kids engaged in community politics than gang warfare!

* * *

I'm trying to be *res-pon-sa-ble, ¿sabes?* I mean, when Father Ronquillo recommended me to the city council to head up the Community Youth Services unit years ago, that was *firme*. It was after the peace treaty and I must admit, it was rough taking that on. What if Louie got pissed off? I didn't want to upset the gang peace we had going. So I sucked it up and told Father Ronquillo, "I'll do it, but I gotta clear it with Louie first." Turns out Louie was cool about it all. "*Aviéntate, vato*," he told me, "I got your back." Soon we're recruiting *vatos* from both gangs into the city youth programs. Together we've turned the gang kids around and headed many of them on the road to college. *¡Órale!* But now we got to deal with these *cabrones* that want to destroy the barrio. No way, dude, you gotta step over me and Louie first, and we ain't gonna let that happen.

* * *

My God, there's a lot of people here. What's this? It's Old Man Baldemar walking up the street pushing a wheelbarrow ahead of him. As he comes closer he recognizes me. "Hello, Yoli, glad to see you back home."

I look down at the wheelbarrow. In it is a heap of items from his house. It only takes me a moment to recognize them—they're the leftover items we dragged from Mrs. Romero's house so many years ago, the items he kept separated from the rest of the lost objects.

"Time to return these to where they belong," he says.

"Wait," I tell him. I pull the tube of xenosium out of my jeans and toss it into the heap. He smiles and walks on.

* * *

Max Martínez, standing next to me, taps me on the shoulder. "Hey, Frank, what do you suppose Old Man Baldemar's up to?"

I turn to where Max is pointing. Yep, it's Old Man Baldemar, all right. He's pushing a wheelbarrow toward Mrs. Romero's house. When he gets to the chain-link fence surrounding it, he dumps the contents of the wheelbarrow onto a heap of trash at the gate. He leaves the wheelbarrow upturned on the heap, turns around and walks back to the crowd with a smile on his face. In all my years at the *Arroyo Grande Gazette*, did I ever see Old Man Baldemar smile? Just then, I hear the crowd begin to murmur. I turn toward the street and see it's the bulldozer drivers. They're climbing onto the bulldozers.

My reporter habits kick in, I note the time the drivers start the engines.

* * *

When the bulldozers start up, our singing stops. I look around at the people near me: the Maldonado brothers and their families, Junior Valdez and his wife, Mrs. Ybarra and Sra. Tanguma, Howard Meltzer, Sam Bedford and, of course, the movie star, the astronaut, the journalist. All of their attention is suddenly focused on the bulldozers, as these lethargic demons suddenly come to life.

Pete Navarro nudges me, "Check it out, Rudy, they're going to start the *pedo*."

I look and, sure enough, the police officers that Captain Bowers brought in from El Paso are lined up shoulder-to-shoulder, twenty of them. They lower their riot masks and proceed to walk toward the crowd gathered in front of Mrs. Romero's house. The first bulldozer, armed with a ripper claw, lumbers behind the line of officers, followed by the other three vehicles, each with enormous blade scoopers held high.

"Are we going to let them do this to our community?" That's Choo Choo shouting to the crowd.

The first bulldozer arrives at the chain-link fence in front of Mrs. Romero's house. The driver raises the ripper claw high over the bulldozer cab and prepares to bring it down on the heap of trash obstructing his way. Suddenly, someone runs in front of the bulldozer and sits down on top of the upturned wheelbarrow on the heap of trash—it's Choo Choo Torres!

* * *

¡Híjole! The moment I see my Choo Choo sit down on the heap of trash, I know what I must do. I run over and join him on the heap. He smiles at me when I settle in next to him. He reaches out and holds my hand. Within moments, we're joined by Jeannie, Junior, Rudy Vargas, Pete Navarro and even Mr. Astronaut himself!

"Ah, come on guys!" the bulldozer driver calls out, "I'm just doing my job!"

"You should be ashamed of yourself! This is our barrio, this is our home!"

* * *

"Send them in, Andy. I want anyone obstructing the demolition arrested. And I don't care if they get hurt."

"Will do," I reply over the walkie. I turn and nod to the sergeant from El Paso, and he motions for his men to go after the people blocking the bulldozer.

* * *

Dear Lord, help us in our time of need. The police are moving toward Choo Choo, Yoli and the others on the trash heap. I don't want my people hurt. I know what I have to do.

"Father O'Keefe," I say, "Come with me. This is why the Lord wanted us here."

* * *

Who's that? Geez, is that Archbishop Ronquillo and Father O'Keefe? Are they really going to join those rabble rousers? Can I even arrest an archbishop? Well, the law is the law, and I've sworn to uphold it. Now, what's this, he's talking to the sergeant.

* * *

The line of police in riot gear comes to a stop in their march toward us. Archbishop Ronquillo is blocking their path. "That won't be necessary, officer," the archbishop tells the officer in charge. For a moment the archbishop and the police sergeant square off, each determined, each silently staring at each other.

Then the archbishop turns to our group at the trash heap—we're a good dozen now. He looks at us and one by one calls out our names. "Choo Choo, Yoli, Reymundo, Bobby, Junior, Rudy, Pete, you all know me and I know all of you. I've known some of you since you were kids and I say this to you. There's no point in you getting beaten up today or arrested. I ask you, please, let this man do his job."

This is what happens when you let Church leaders rule your life. They actually think they have the right to make decisions for you—just like the boys at NASA. Don't you think I know what I'm doing when I go out into space or sit down in front of a bulldozer? Whose side is Ronquillo on, anyway?

* * *

Heck, if I were still on the Arroyo Grande police force, I'd probably be standing next to those El Paso cops instead of here on this heap of trash. But it's right that I be here This is where I belong—at least I've learned *that* from Jeannie and the others at the Pirámide. But what is Father Ronquillo saying?

* * *

This is a tough one, I know we're in the right, and the others have followed my move, especially Yoli. Yes, we all know we'll probably be beat up and arrested. But we're all ready for that. Now here's Father Ronquillo pulling a guilt trip on all of us. One thing for sure, I gotta think of the bigger picture, not just the heroics of this day. I have to show leadership.

* * *

Why is my Choo Choo standing up? He turns to me. "Yoli, we made our point. They've won this battle. We got a long war ahead of us. There'll be more battles to be fought."

With that, he takes my hand and begins to lead me back to the crowd. I stop walking and hold my ground. He turns to me. He won't let go of my hand.

"Yoli, I don't want you hurt. I don't want any of us to get hurt. These bastards have all the marbles right now, but there's other ways of winning." He lets go of my hand, turns and walks away.

Jeannie joins me then, looking at me in disbelief. "Really?"

I turn to her and nod.

"*Pensándolo bien*, Jeannie, I think Choo Choo's right on this one."

* * *

Damn Priest is not as dumb as he looks. Got those troublemakers to back down. Great! They're all walking back to the crowd. Now we can get the demolition going, and I won't have to spend the day doing arrest paperwork. I pick up the walkie and push the talk button, "Andy, tell the bulldozer driver to continue."

* * *

I look around at the crowd around me. Some people are really pissed off at me. "Why'd you chicken out, Choo Choo?"

"Choo Choo, how could you let us down?"

I don't say anything. Sometimes, words don't mean anything anyway.

* * *

Old Man Baldemar comes up to me and smiles. "All is not lost, Yoli."

Yeah, I'm thinking, tell that to the people whose homes are about to be demolished. Tell that to my mom and dad. I watch in fascinated horror as the driver in the lead bulldozer lifts the ripper arm up and sends it crashing down on the heap of trash. He does it once, twice, three times. Then he turns the bulldozer to the chain-link fence and begins to tear at the fencing.

Why has he stopped? He's looking down at the heap of trash. He turns off the bulldozer's engine as if trying to listen to something.

What is that sound? A rumble. Coming from . . . the ground.

Suddenly everyone in the crowd can hear it. A low rumble that soon begins to shake the ground underneath us. What the heck is it? We've never had an earthquake in Arroyo Grande.

With a thunderous whoosh, a jet of water erupts from under the trash heap, sending water, trash and parched grass dancing twelve feet into the air.

I can't believe my eyes! It's a gusher just like the one that erupted in Mrs. Romero's front yard so long ago!

* * *

"Harold, what the hell is going on?"

"That idiot bulldozer driver must have hit a water main. Jonathan, I'm going to fire him for this!"

* * *

¡Híjole! I can't believe my eyes. That heap of trash in front of Mrs. Romero's is sinking into a hole where the sidewalk used to be. The sidewalk just caved in! Whoa, are we looking at another sinkhole?

"Sinkhole!" The word quickly spreads through the crowd.

"*Es un milagro,*" Mrs. Ybarra shouts out. Of course, she would.

"Oh, Choo Choo. Look!" I say, pointing to where we were sitting just a few minutes ago.

The trash heap is completely gone. Yeah, that hole is definitely getting bigger. The water keeps gushing out and just as quickly begins to fill up the ever widening sinkhole. I look at the people standing around me. They're having trouble believing what their eyes tell them.

* * *

"Look, over there!"

It's Rudy Vargas pointing down the street, where another gusher has erupted in the middle of Calle Cuatro. Man, this is better than any script I've ever read or movie I've been in—look, there's yet another geyser blowing off in front of what used to be the Alaníz home.

* * *

"Harold, what the hell are we going to do?"

"Shut up, Jonathan. Let me think."

"How're we gonna demolish the houses?"

"I said shut up!"

* * *

Will you look at that! Water is cascading from more than a dozen gushers that have spouted along Calle Cuatro, some in driveways, some in front lawns, some in the middle of the street. Just as quickly, the water pours into the street and turns it into a river.

The water coursing down the street is emptying into the largest of the sinkholes in the middle of Calle Cuatro. And the sinkhole is beginning to fill up, forming a large pool of water.

Oh, this is mighty, mighty wonderful! Now I'm counting fifteen geysers all up and down Calle Cuatro. What a sight! What a sight!

* * *

¡Híjole! There's geysers breaking out on Calle Cinco as well! Sure enough, I can see past Mrs. Romero's house and into the back yard fence where I can see a fountain of water glistening in the sun on Calle Tres.

* * *

The street's getting completely flooded, and my safety training kicks in. "Move back folks, move away from the street. We don't want you washed away. Señora Tanguma, let me help you."

* * *

Look at that! A minute ago Bobby Hernández was ready to get arrested. Now he's showing Bowers and his men that cops should be helping our people and not arresting them. You can take Bobby out of the police force, but I guess you can't take the cop out of old Bobby.

Here comes Choo Choo and Yoli running up to me.

"Max! Is this what I think it is? Doesn't look like a broken water line to me!"

"Aquifer," I reply.

"I knew it!"

"That's the only thing that could produce all this water. Arroyo Grande is living up to its name. We're sitting on top of an aquifer that's broken through to the surface."

"That means . . . ?"

* * *

"Harold, we can't demolish these houses in all this water. We'll have to tell the work crews to come back tomorrow. Wait till the water subsides."

"Jonathan, sometimes you can be really stupid. The problem is much worse than that!"

"Huh?"

"That's not a broken water line. Not that much water. It's an aquifer, idiot! There's an aquifer under Arroyo Grande. There must be some kind of funnel that's bringing all that water to the surface. No point in demolishing the houses now."

"What?"

"Idiot, ever try building a casino on a foundation that's undermined by water?"

"Can't we drain it? I mean, let's get engineers on it!"

"Jonathan, it's not the construction logistics. It's the insurance! Insurance will never cover us building on such unstable land. We're done with the Arroyo Grande casino project. It's over!"

* * *

"Yep, the insurance folks will never insure a casino or any other structure built on such unstable ground," I tell Max and Yoli.

"Oh, Choo Choo, that means we've won!" Yoli says beaming. Then she notices I'm staring at something. "What is it, Choo Cho?"

She and Max turn their eyes to where I am looking—Mrs. Romero's house. There on the porch stands Mrs. Romero with Don Sabastiano and Peanuts. The elderly couple wave at us.

"Yes, we've won," I tell Yoli and Max. "The question is, what do we do next?"

AND THEN

A loud crack from the beamed recesses of Mrs. Romero's old house awakened Yoli Mendoza. She turned in bed and saw Choo Choo still fast asleep, his trusty handcam resting on the end table next to the plaster of paris Admiral Dewey lamp that he had pulled from a watery sinkhole a lifetime ago.

Quietly, Yoli got out of bed, put on the white terrycloth robe given to her by her neighbor Rosalinda Rodríguez. She walked over to the crib and looked down at the sleeping baby. It was their first child, all of three months old. They had named him Rudy, after a good friend who had met an early death but whose memory was forever with them.

Yoli adjusted the blanket to fully cover the sleeping child and then proceeded into the adjacent hallway. The feel of the polished wood floor was cool on her bare feet as she made her way past the many paintings, celebrity photos and awards that evidenced the remarkable careers of a celebrated artist and an equally acclaimed filmmaker.

Yoli entered the renovated kitchen, where Mrs. Romero once had baked an unusual wedding cake. She reheated the coffee from the day before in the microwave oven—she was addicted to day-old coffee. She added her habitual teaspoon of sugar, then took the steaming cup out to the front porch and sat down in the old-style swing that Choo Choo had installed a year ago.

She took in the view. Downslope from the house, where a white picket fence once stood, waves of water lapped onto the sandy shore.

The view of the sun rising over Lake Arroyo Grande was stunning.

"Always pretty, isn't it?"

It was Choo Choo who had walked onto the porch, rubbing sleep out of his eyes.

"Sure is. I'll miss this."

"We're making the right decision."

Later that day, Choo Choo would be off to his new job in Arizona, leaving behind a Hollywood career for something more important, to head up the media arm of Pirámide Enterprises. Yoli would follow in a few weeks with the baby. She would take up *her* new role as artistic director of the sprawling pyramid construction in the Arizona desert.

"The future is now," Choo Choo said.

Also by Jesús Salvador Treviño

Eyewitness: A Filmmaker's Memoir of the Chicano Movement

The Fabulous Sinkhole and Other Stories

The Skyscraper that Flew and Other Stories